A strangled choking sound had him spinning around.

Jo had backed out by the time he crouched beside her.

"Oh, dear God," she whispered hoarsely. "Oh, dear God." She seemed unable to tear her eyes from the darkness beyond her headlamp beam.

Alan grasped her shoulders and turned her. "What?"

Her throat worked, her gaze now fastened desperately on him. "Bones," she finally managed.

"A skeleton?"

Her teeth chattered. "More than one."

"Damn it." He tugged her closer and wrapped her in a tight embrace. She burrowed in and shook but didn't cry. The tough woman he'd gotten to know, the one determined to face the nightmare from her past, wouldn't let herself cry.

Then he eased her back and said, "Let me look."

WHAT IS HIDDEN

USA TODAY Bestselling Author

JANICE KAY JOHNSON

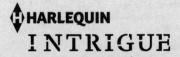

HARLEQUIN
INTRIGUE

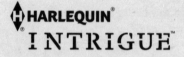

Recycling programs
for this product may
not exist in your area.

ISBN-13: 978-1-335-58239-3

What Is Hidden

Harlequin Enterprises ULC
22 Adelaide St. West, 41st Floor
Toronto, Ontario M5H 4E3, Canada
www.Harlequin.com

Printed in U.S.A.

An author of more than ninety books for children and adults with more than seventy-five for Harlequin, **Janice Kay Johnson** writes about love and family and pens books of gripping romantic suspense. A *USA TODAY* bestselling author and an eight-time finalist for the Romance Writers of America RITA® Award, she won a RITA® Award in 2008. A former librarian, Janice raised two daughters in a small town north of Seattle, Washington.

Books by Janice Kay Johnson

Harlequin Intrigue

Hide the Child
Trusting the Sheriff
Within Range
Brace for Impact
The Hunting Season
The Last Resort
Cold Case Flashbacks
Dead in the Water
Mustang Creek Manhunt
What Is Hidden

Visit the Author Profile page at Harlequin.com.

CAST OF CHARACTERS

Josephine Summerlin—Jo promises to spend the summer working in the magnificent limestone cavern owned by her stepdad—and to quiet her teenage half sister's wild rebellion. Only it may not be that simple.

Alan Burke—A former navy SEAL and police detective home temporarily, he's a loner disdained by the locals—until his particular skills prove essential to find several missing women.

Rod Summerlin—Raising three kids after his wife abandoned them all wasn't easy. Now he figures his stepdaughter owes him. She can make his rebellious teenage daughter see sense. A human skull found in a back passage of the cavern? Ridiculous—and bad for the cavern's reputation.

Lucy Summerlin—Sixteen years old, Lucy wants to believe her dad, but she *knows* her friend didn't lie about seeing that skull.

Brody Summerlin—Just like his dad, he's all about the family cavern. He's torn up when his former girlfriend goes missing—and to realize *he* might be a suspect.

Andrew Frazier—The local deputy alone connects Amy Kendall's disappearance with the abduction of other women in recent years. Does he want to find proof he's right?

Prologue

The lighting in this parking lot sucked. She hadn't noticed on her way into the tavern. *Then* she'd been feeling sophisticated, a grown woman confident enough to saunter into a bar on her own. Now her forehead crinkled in puzzlement as she tried to remember where she'd left her car. Wow—she had to be a little bit drunk.

Oh, wait. Her keys were in her hand. *Press button on fob.* And—taillights flashed off to one side. Who knew? She was a genius, right? Or not really drunk. Or…

Of course, she fumbled with the keys as she opened her car door, and they fell to the ground. Wonderful. It was so blasted *dark* over here. Why hadn't she picked a tavern that planned for somewhat pickled customers to be able to find dropped keys? But there they were, and she got in behind the wheel. Then it took her a minute to insert the key in the ignition and to lay her hand on the seatbelt clip. It was important to wear a seatbelt, she told herself with a serious nod. Especially when she'd been drinking.

Which was totally all right, since this was her twenty-first birthday. Her friends at school had held a party for her yesterday, and her parents were expecting her tomorrow and would undoubtedly "surprise" her with a cake, candles and gifts. They didn't know she'd decided to head home this afternoon. *She'd* surprise them. Home wasn't even an hour away.

As she sat there, a weird feeling came over her, the fingers tiptoeing down her back kind, making her look around uneasily. Well, no wonder; with the overhead light on and that damned dark parking lot, she was on display. If somebody was watching, they were probably just trying to decide why she was just sitting there.

She fired up the engine and heard all the locks *snick*. A moment later, she pulled out on the narrow highway, so familiar from drives to the big city—Springfield. She giggled at the thought, then noticed she'd crossed the center line. Oops! Fortunately, there was hardly any other traffic, only headlights that had appeared quite a way behind her.

She'd like to think she'd sobered up some by the time she turned off the highway onto a narrower one, more a country road, even though it, too, had a yellow stripe down the middle. Hardly any shoulder, though, and awfully dark. Not like she wasn't used to it; her parents had acreage several miles outside town, and she'd been taught to drive super carefully, especially at night, because deer and coyotes and other wildlife often crossed the road right in front of a car without realizing the danger.

On her dashboard, a red light caught her eye. When had *that* come on? She had no idea what it was trying to tell her, but it probably wasn't good. She might be imagining a faint burning smell, but… Yes, she should pull over and call her dad to come and get her.

There wasn't any way to really get off the road, but she braked anyway, and was proud of herself when she managed to switch on the warning lights. Oh, and she should probably turn off the engine, in case the oil was perilously low or something like that.

She groped in her purse on the passenger side. Her phone wasn't in the outside pocket where she usually carried it. "*Where, oh, where,*" she half sang as her searching fingers found her wallet, a small cosmetics bag, receipts, a tissue packet. Something hard… no, that was her electronic reader. *Where, oh, where…*

A picture appeared before her. Her sitting on a barstool, chatting with several guys, including the kind of cute bartender. Phone lying there; she'd almost decided to text her parents instead of surprising them. Then she'd accepted another refill, and… Couldn't remember another thing.

Oh, God—had she left her phone behind at the tavern? Once she was home, she could call and they'd surely have it, but…unless someone came along to give her a lift, she'd have to hoof it. Which wouldn't kill her—it probably wasn't more than a couple miles to go, but the near-complete darkness gave her the creeps. None of the local wildlife attacked *people*, as far as she knew, except maybe a mama black bear with cubs, and it *was* spring.

And then—oh, thank you, God—headlights appeared in her rearview mirror. Given how remote this was, the driver just about had to be a neighbor. Someone she knew. The lights were high, almost blinding her in the mirror, which meant it was a pickup. Practically everybody hereabouts drove pickups.

A turn signal came on, and the truck pulled up behind her. Its flashers came on, too, and she watched in her side mirror as the driver's side door opened and someone—a man—got out and walked forward.

Bulky shoulders in a well-worn jean jacket. She couldn't really see his face even when he stopped beside her door and made a twirling motion with one finger. Only she couldn't roll down the window without turning the engine back on, so maybe it would be better if she just opened the door.

She had it open, and he'd gripped the top of it and leaned down before she did see him…and recognized him. He'd been at the tavern, on the barstool right beside her. He'd flirted with her, but not in a way that scared her. It had to be just chance that he lived out this way, too, didn't it?

But then he smiled, and dread filled her.

"You got a little farther down the road than I expected before your engine conked out," he remarked, "but practice makes perfect. And since you didn't get all the way home…"

His hand fisted and he swung at her. Pain exploded in her cheek and temple. As she slammed into the steering wheel and true darkness engulfed her, her last thought was a desperate plea.

Mommy. Daddy.

Chapter One

"We need you."

Thanks to the memory of her stepfather's plea, guilt rode along with Jo Summerlin during the entire drive from her home in Illinois to southern Missouri where she'd grown up. She might as well have buckled it into the passenger seat beside her. And however she tried to justify herself, that sense of guilt wouldn't shut up.

As if this internal argument/justification was anything new.

Still, she couldn't help thinking, *This is my fault. I was practically Lucy's mother, and I abandoned her.*

Except, she *wasn't* her half sister's mother. Yes, Jo had stepped in when their mother walked out on them all: her husband and three children. Jo hadn't had any choice, though she'd been a kid herself, only thirteen.

Still, would it have killed her to stay closer for college? Gotten a job locally? Even lived at home for a few more years?

She left the freeway for a highway, then another one. Roads became narrower; this last one had a yellow stripe down the middle, but nobody with any common sense would exceed the forty-mile-an-hour speed limit.

Jo hadn't passed a single other car since she began the climb that took the road along the steep hillside above the river. The water was running especially high, she couldn't help noting, not surprising after the unusually wet spring. To her left, just on the other side of the guardrail, the land dropped precipitously. To her right, trees cloaked in the vivid green of new leaves somehow clung to the rocky, equally steep hillside.

Spring. Well, technically summer, but still. For the first time all day, Jo felt genuine anticipation. The countryside in the Ozarks was gorgeous, only the vivid fall foliage eclipsing springtime.

The sight of the garish billboard ahead that read SUMMERLIN CAVERN had her making a face without even thinking about it. She'd argued for using the billboards on state highways but going for something more tasteful in this wooded setting. She'd lost. As always.

Taking the familiar turnoff, Jo ordered herself to think positive. Being home for the summer might be fun. And she really would be glad to spend more time with Brody and Lucy, if it wasn't too late. Teenage Lucy and Brody, almost twenty-one, might be too busy with friends to care if Jo was around or not.

Time to quit beating herself up. She'd stayed in close touch with her siblings; the three of them texted regularly, shared photos and occasionally talked on the phone. Lucy had come to stay with her a few times—when her dad could "spare" her. Jo came home for most major holidays. No, she hadn't made it since Christmas, six months ago, but Lucy hadn't gone off the rails now because big sister wasn't around. She might have been quiet lately. Caught up in the final weeks of the school year; Jo hadn't noticed any new distance, though— not until Jo's stepfather had called to beg her to come home to "do something about" Lucy, his frustration and bewilderment bleeding through every word of that phone conversation.

She'd teased him by saying, "You know, I spoiled you. I was such an angel."

A brief silence. Then he burst into laughter. "You're right. Never a moment of defiance."

That might be putting it a *little* too strongly. She laughed, too, although it's true that she'd been an exceptionally well-behaved teenager, too afraid of abandonment after losing her mother to be anything else.

The last thing her stepfather said was, "Whatever is going on with Lucy isn't rebellion. It's—" he hesitated for a long moment before finishing "—anger. Or fear."

What could have happened? At Christmas everything had been…well, not smooth, there were always undercurrents with this family, but fine. Normal. Brody was a jerk, but probably no more so than most guys strutting into new adulthood. Lucy had been given to rolling her eyes and mumbling lines she refused to repeat loud enough for Rod to hear, but wasn't that normal for a teenage girl who had to defy her dad somehow?

Well, Jo was determined to get to the bottom of this. She hadn't been home for an entire summer since she'd graduated from college. Rod had somehow conned her into agreeing not just to a visit, but to work, just as she had during high school and college breaks. Really, what else would she do with herself? At least there'd be no learning curve since she'd worked in the family business most of her weekends and after-school hours since she was twelve or so.

But this time, it was for her sister's sake.

A final curve, and a stunning vista opened in front of her. More stunning if an extensive parking lot hadn't been blasted out of the hillside, but at least the building that housed the gift and coffee shop had been built of the same gray stone that formed the bones of the hill and tumbled into the river.

The enormous half-open mouth of the cavern yawned in the hillside. Summerlin Cavern, open six days a week for tours. Jo had led hundreds—no, thousands of them. She'd been the barista; she'd operated the cash register in the gift shop where tourists also bought tickets for the tours. Her stepfather kept the cavern profitable by hiring help as little as possible, and as young as Jo had been after the divorce, she'd already been a useful part of the operation.

Which was maybe a slightly cynical way to look at the truth that Rod had stepped up to raise her as his own.

There were enough cars parked in the lot to suggest a tour was underway, but her experienced eye told her there couldn't be many people waiting for the next tour. That wouldn't please Rod. She'd have to remind him that school had barely let out for some districts—

including the one in Illinois where she taught—and probably some had yet to finish for the year. Business would pick up drastically by July.

She drove on by the parking lot, taking a narrow road, marked No Trespassing. Around a last curve, just out of sight of the cavern entrance, a white-painted two-story house clung to a patch of ground barely wide enough for the foundation and a garage. From this narrow perch on a cliff, plank stairs led down to a dock on the river. Home since she was a kid, when her mother married Rodney Summerlin.

Jo made a face. Her six-year-old self had been okay with a stepfather, but she remembered all too well her first sight of the cavern opening. It had terrified her. She'd had nightmares about that cave for months. Rod's exasperation wasn't surprising. He loved the cavern named for his family. Other well-known show caverns in Missouri had names like Fantastic Caverns, Devil's Well, Talking Rocks Cavern, Bridal Cave. Forget that. Rod Summerlin had inherited the land and everything that lay beneath the ground from his father, who had inherited it from *his* father. Part of the tour spiel included family history, somewhat exaggerated. He wouldn't have it any other way.

When, at about Lucy's age, Jo got enthusiastic plotting how they could raise interest in the cavern, she'd announced they needed more highway billboards, and a new name. Something spectacular. Rod had not reacted well.

Braking in front of the house, Jo realized she was rolling her eyes, but also grinning at the memory.

Rusty, the family dog, raced around from the back barking furiously. A stray who'd showed up a couple of years ago, he was maybe part Labrador but had a scruffy rust-brown coat and eyes of two different colors. Jo found him endearing, but no one could call him handsome.

Once she got out of her car, Rusty must have recognized her from her last visit, because he jumped at her trying to lick her face. After some petting, she slung her purse and laptop bag over her shoulder, and lifted a sizeable suitcase from the trunk. Why hadn't Rusty's racket brought Lucy out? She was surely home by now. Wasn't this the last week of school locally? There weren't likely to be any after-school activities this late in the year.

Jo outright snorted. She couldn't remember Lucy ever doing theater or yearbook or whatever. Rod had always favored his son. Brody had been permitted to play high school sports—football in the fall and baseball in the spring—but Jo had managed one season of volleyball as a freshman only by begging rides home from other parents. She'd given up after that. Even though she wasn't his real daughter, Jo was supposed to be as dedicated to promoting the great and glorious Summerlin Cavern as Rod was.

Well, she'd do her part this summer, for Lucy, but also because she did admire Rod's dedication. This was among the most extensive and impressive caverns in a state that boasted well over seven thousand of them.

Tour guides were top-notch, and people never left feeling anything less than awestruck.

Also, Jo had to admit, she owed her stepfather. After Mom ditched the family, he hadn't been obligated to keep Jo and raise her as his own, but he had. There was no question of whether she'd help now that he needed it.

Heck, it occurred to her, Lucy was probably leading the current tour or stuck in the gift shop behind the espresso machine or the cash register.

Jo hauled her stuff up the steps onto the porch that stretched the width of the house and let herself in with her key, shutting the door on a woeful dog.

"Anyone home?" she called, just in case.

"Jo?" The voice floated from the bedrooms above. "Is that you?"

"Who else?"

The pretty teenager came rushing downstairs and cast herself into her big sister's arms. "You're here! I didn't believe Dad when he said you were coming! You're not really staying all summer, are you?"

Laughing, Jo said, "I'm afraid so. He didn't see why I should laze around for three months when I could be making myself useful here."

Lucy pulled back, her delight having vanished into resentment. The change was shockingly abrupt. "Baby-sitting *me*, you mean."

"I'm excited to spend time with you." Jo didn't want to directly lie and say, *No, he didn't say anything about you*.

"Sure. Well, I'm *fine!*" she exclaimed. "He just doesn't

like me doing stuff with friends. *Brody* can go out and party whenever *he* wants, but *me*? *I* have a *curfew*."

Since she was sixteen while her brother was just short of his twenty-first birthday, Jo could sympathize with Rod even if she, too, had been mad at him half the time until she escaped to college. Still, the drama seemed excessive.

Jo smiled. "The two of us can flee when we feel like it and go do stuff."

"You mean, you'll keep me busy so I don't have *time* for my friends." Lucy backed up, her expression ugly. "I'm not *dumb*, you know, and I don't have to listen to *you*." She whirled and tore up the stairs as fast as she'd come down. A moment later, a door slammed.

Jo gaped at the empty hall above. She hadn't forgotten her own tumultuous moods, mostly around the time she turned thirteen, although she had had plenty of excuses. But Lucy had turned sixteen in April. She should be past the stage of excessive hormones, shouldn't she? She *was* past it. She and Jo had had fun during Christmas break.

Why blast me, Jo wondered, *if Lucy was mostly mad at her dad? Please don't let her be pregnant. Or...*

Getting into drugs?

Mood squelched, Jo dragged her suitcase upstairs to her old bedroom, unchanged from when she left for college at eighteen. Maybe if she updated it this summer, she wouldn't so easily slip into feeling like the kid she'd been then.

But she shrugged off the idea. Maybe she'd walk over to the gift shop and say hi to Rod and Brody when they had a free moment. To Austin, too—he'd worked full-time for the Summerlins for the entire ten years since she left for college. Would he hit on her again this summer?

THREE DAYS LATER, Jo regretted her ready agreement to come home. It felt…strange, to be back, sleeping in her childhood bedroom. Her sleep wasn't easy. The mattress had been a cheap one to start with, and now sagged enough that she kept catching herself just before she rolled off the bed. Then, last night, Rusty got excited about something and barked up a storm. The barking receded, as if he was chasing something, then gained in volume. What, did he want one of them to boost him up a cliff to convince that squirrel to descend within reach? Brody yelled out the window, to no effect. Rod must have gone downstairs, because she'd heard him swearing at the "damn dog" before letting him in.

She'd discovered that Rod and Brody believed she had assumed all household tasks, starting with cooking and cleaning the kitchen. That might be her fault, because she'd been so eager to contribute during her previous, much shorter visits. But for three months? No.

To top it all off, she was getting absolutely nowhere with Lucy. The most open communication they'd had was yesterday when Lucy had cried, "Things have just been weird, okay?" Of course, she'd immediately raced upstairs and slammed her bedroom door.

Weird *how*?

The question still on her mind, Jo asked her brother

when they both happened to be in the gift shop this afternoon at a rare, quiet moment. Brody walked with a swagger and looked a lot like his dad: just under six feet, stocky and strong, with sandy-colored hair and brown eyes. He had wandered over to her cash register.

"Weird?" he repeated. "I don't know what she's talking about. She's just flipped out lately." He sneered. "Maybe it's a guy or something."

The fact that he didn't seem to want to meet Jo's eyes gave her a stir of unease.

Brody was *sounding* more like his father every day, too. She hoped she was imagining the way he treated his sister, as if she wasn't worth much. So far, he at least pretended to respect Jo.

"Rusty was sure worked up about something last night."

"Still was this morning. I had to lock him up at home. He's not the sharpest knife in the drawer."

Probably not.

"You didn't say whether you're planning to go back to school in the fall," she commented, as much to change the subject as anything. He'd finished his second year at Missouri State University in Springfield, commuting from home, but then decided to take a year off. She felt sure he'd have had a lot more fun and been more engaged if he'd roomed on campus, but he hadn't fought that battle as successfully as Jo had. In retrospect, she suspected he hadn't cared one way or the other.

He gave a careless shrug. "Probably not. We're so busy here. I have to learn the business since it'll be mine someday."

"Is that what you want?" she asked.

He looked at her like she was nuts. "Why wouldn't I?"

Oh, because there was a big, wide world out there? But she smiled. "Just asking."

"I probably wouldn't have gone at all if it weren't for you," he said, and he wasn't thanking her. "It was a waste of time, just like Dad said."

She kept her voice mild. "Depends on what you want out of life."

"I want to open more of the cave to tours," he burst out. "Advertise. Why shouldn't Summerlin be as well known as Meramec or Onondage? Have you heard about the wild tour the Smallin Civil War Cave offers? They take people adventuring in some of the passages that don't have paved paths and lights. Why can't we do that, too? Some of the best chambers are—"

They paused so Jo could ring up the purchase of a handful of polished multicolored minerals and poured them into a small brown paper bag that said Summerlin Cavern beneath a curving line that suggested the arch of the mouth. The mother and girl—ten or eleven, maybe?—beamed when she asked if they'd enjoyed the tour.

"It was amazing," the mother declared.

Jo waited until the double glass doors closed behind them before she resumed the conversation with her brother. "Did you ask Rod about it?"

"He said it was too dangerous." Brody got the sullen look that she particularly disliked. "I said I'd lead them. I know what I'm doing!"

"You do. Have you done any more exploring?"

The shrug was sulky, too. "He doesn't want me to."

There was speculation that many, if not most, of the caves in Missouri were linked. She knew for a fact that passages in the Summerlin Cavern exited at a somewhat smaller opening on neighboring property. The water that had formed the limestone caverns would have found many crevices to eventually join the streams and river. As a girl, she'd made the trip from that opening to exit at their own end of the cavern, as well as venturing into a few other passages, some opening into spectacular rooms with high ceilings and distinctive formations. Back then, Rod had argued that a one-hour tour was the standard, and most people wouldn't want more than that. She hadn't been able to argue, but she also had some sympathy for Brody's schemes. At least he knew he'd eventually inherit the cavern from his father and be able to do whatever he wanted.

Maybe the assumption it would one day all be his had something to do with Lucy's anger. Rod's belief that women and girls were second-class citizens was pretty obvious.

"I hear voices," Jo said.

Brody pulled out his phone and glanced at it. "Yeah, tour should be letting out. Here come some people from the parking lot, too."

Jo got busy selling tickets for the next tour even as she was aware of the group that had been on the last one spreading out through the extensive gift shop, some talking excitedly, all oohing and aahing at the available merchandise.

Rod's marketing here was effective, from T-shirts and sweatshirts as well as postcards that said Summerlin Cavern with a close-up of one of the extraordinary columns, stalactites, stalagmites and flowstones that were such wondrous sights deep in the cave, to a huge selection of polished and raw rocks and minerals as well as some carved into bookends, boxes and beads and pennants for jewelry. Local crafts did well here, too: hand-woven baskets, carved wood, artwork and pottery. She did a brisk business ringing up purchases, wrapping them carefully and handing them over with a smile in between selling tickets.

Austin, who had led the most recent tour, grinned the moment he saw Jo. Yes, he'd already asked her out, but shrugged blithely when she said, "Gee, no thanks."

From what Brody and Rod had told her, the lanky guy in his thirties never suffered from lack of female companionship. She smiled wryly in return before greeting the next customer.

Rod had been back in the offices doing his book-keeping or ordering or whatever. Now he began to circulate with a geniality and pride that drew people to him.

The next tour was to be led by Brody, with Austin probably slated for the following one. He was the only full-time employee right now. Besides, of course, Rod, Jo and Brody, with Lucy slated to be full-time, too, for the summer. Jo hadn't been here twenty-four hours when Rod started including her in the tour rotation. A couple of college students usually worked here summers, too, and part-timers filled in as he grudgingly needed them.

Brody edged over to her again. "Do you know where Lucy is? Dad has that slitty-eyed look."

Jo glanced his way. Yes, indeed, he was rotating in place to scan the room with barely veiled irritation.

"No, is she even home from school?"

"She's supposed to be."

Jo smiled at the next person in line just as she saw her sister rush in from the outside, cell phone clutched in her hand.

Spotting Brody and Jo, she hurried to them, her expression distraught. "Autumn just called! Did you hear?"

"You'd better hide that phone and get to work," her brother said. "Dad wants you to take over the espresso—"

"Listen to me!" she cried, voice shrill enough to carry. People started to turn. "It's Amy Kendall this time! She's gone, and the police don't even care!"

Gone? This time? Jo wondered what nobody in the family had bothered to tell her about.

Rod bulled his way through the gathering cluster as Jo hastily boxed a gorgeous pair of earrings.

"We don't have time to stand around gossiping," he said, keeping his own voice down. "This is a bad time—"

"You never listen," Lucy spat. "Amy Kendall has disappeared, and everyone is saying something bad has to have happened. She'd never take off on her own."

"Am I supposed to know who this girl is?" Rod asked, with ill-concealed impatience.

"Yes!" Lucy dashed at tears that had started to run down her cheeks. "She was Brody's girlfriend."

Jo saw the shock on her brother's face even as she absorbed her own dose. "I used to babysit her," she heard herself say slowly. "Remember? Amy and her sister Caroline." Amy had been a year ahead of Brody in school, if she remembered right, which would make her almost twenty-two. She was a beauty the last time Jo saw her—dark, straight, shiny hair that practically reached her butt and swayed with her every move, long legs and slender body, and startling eyes that had made Jo think of amber.

"Excuse me," a man said loudly. "We don't want to miss the tour. Can we buy our tickets?"

Rod shook himself. "We'll talk about this later. The police know what they're doing. We need to concentrate on *our* jobs right now."

He was right, Jo thought, although she was shaken enough that she wouldn't be able to think about anything but the young woman she'd known, who might be in deep trouble.

And…*this time*? Was Amy not the first young woman to go missing?

Chapter Two

Alan Burke drove the last nail into the back porch step he was replacing. Both the sweltering-hot Missouri sun and bitterly cold Missouri winters were hard on wood. This house had sat empty for too many years now. The interior needed a lot of work, too—more than he might bother to do—but fixing up the exterior was essential if he intended to sell the place. The exertion quieted the unrest inside him, too.

No matter what, he had to do something with his days besides work out in the weight room he'd set up in what had once been a dining room in the house where he'd lived until his mother sent him away. Giving himself too much time to brood wasn't healthy. He'd done his job as well as he could. Trusting that he could ever rely on others in the same way again, though, that was something else.

He bounced experimentally on all three steps, feeling no give. Good enough. Might as well stain them this afternoon—

The growl of an engine—pickup truck or SUV, he thought—coming up the nearly mile-long gravel driveway made his muscles tighten in an instinctive need to be combat ready. *Dial it down*, he told himself. What he should be was irritated; he hadn't ordered anything lately, so this couldn't be a postal worker or delivery service. On the few occasions he'd been recognized in town he hadn't been subtle about his preference not to be bothered.

Alan gave thought to staying where he was, or even going inside and ignoring any knock on the front door, but finally growled under his breath and stalked around the house, hammer still in his hand.

Being completely unarmed didn't sit well with him.

SUV—navy blue with a white and red insignia on the side as well as a rack of lights on the roof. Sheriff's deputy. What, someone was checking to be sure he hadn't taken up his old man's trade?

The driver's side door slammed closed, and a cop appeared around the front, eyes on Alan. Lean guy, light brown hair, dark glasses. And familiar, although it took Alan a minute.

"Drew?"

Andrew Frazier had been his best friend when they were boys, but after so many years, he didn't think he'd have recognized the guy if they'd happened to pass anywhere else in the world. But here? Had to be.

The deputy took off the dark glasses and grinned. "Damn. It really is you."

Alan made a noncommittal sound in his throat. He wasn't so sure the man hiding out in the backwoods of Missouri was anyone even he knew, much less a grown version of the outwardly cocky boy he'd been, the one who never let anyone see how bad things were at home.

"Didn't know you were still around," he said, grudgingly polite.

The two of them had had good times, both a little wild for different reasons. They'd been driven to explore the extensive cave systems rife in this part of Missouri. Not that either had mentioned their hobby to their parents.

"I did an enlistment in the army, then college." Drew's shoulders moved. "Came home for a visit, ran into my high school girlfriend, *bam*. Have two kids now. Take it you're not married?"

"I don't think there's a woman alive who'd put up with me these days." He hesitated. He wouldn't have even considered inviting anyone else to come into the house, but this seemed unavoidable. "Can I offer you a beer? Or a cup of coffee?"

Drew's face tightened. "Not a beer. I'm on the clock. I'd have made it out here to say hi one of these days anyway, but I'm here now because I'm hoping you can help out tomorrow, as close to first light as we can make it."

Alan didn't like the sound of that, but only dipped his head and led the way up onto the front porch he'd replaced last week, and inside. Drew's head turned as they passed the weight room, but Alan didn't stop until he reached the kitchen. It was ugly as hell—*dated* didn't even begin to describe a room caught in a major time warp—but at least it was clean.

Alan had made a pitcher of lemonade earlier, and

poured them both glasses instead of brewing coffee.
They sat at the battered kitchen table on the only two
chairs—picked up at a thrift store—and looked at each
other.

"Your grandmother came back to bury your mom,"
Drew said after a minute. "Told me you'd gone into
the navy."

"That's right."

"Later, there was talk you'd become a SEAL."

"I suppose Grandma stayed in touch with someone
in town." He let his tone become sardonic. "I'm surprised anyone believed that story, everybody being
so sure I'd end up no better than my father." Dad had
manufactured meth, sometimes using the caves to hide
his operation.

"You really were a SEAL?"

The urgency in the question made Alan curious.
"Yeah. I stayed in until I didn't make it back far enough
from an injury to return to active duty." He hid his disquiet. "What's this about?"

His friend let out a long breath and scrubbed a hand
over his face. "We've got a young woman missing."

Shocked, Alan rocked forward, his chair scraping.
"Are you looking at *me*?"

"No, no! We need manpower to search, and I'm
thinking you might have skills we can use. You know
what it's like. In a county as rural as this one, we don't
have anywhere near the numbers we need for any serious search and rescue. We're organizing volunteers,
but they're not always as useful as they want to think
they are."

Settling back into the chair, Alan nodded his under-standing. "What makes you think this woman didn't just take off?"

"Sheriff thinks that's what happened, but I'm push-ing hard for us to take this seriously." He paused. "Thing is, turns out several other young women have gone missing in the past few years. Might be some even earlier, but that's harder to determine. Nobody tied them together, because this was over a three-county area. And you know how it is. They were all at least twenty-one. With adults, law enforcement wants to believe they'll come home on their own when they're ready."

Alan nodded. He knew.

"Only none of them ever did. I didn't like what I heard about the one who vanished from Douglas County three years ago, but she wasn't in our jurisdiction."

And cops were usually too busy to follow up when the crime wasn't their responsibility. Too much else usually was.

"Nagged at me, you know? Her friends and fam-ily all said she wouldn't have done anything like that. She had a boyfriend and a summer job lined up." He shook his head. "Then we got the call this morning. Girl named Amy Kendall, almost twenty-two, left a kegger last night. She'd driven herself, set off for home by herself. Never arrived."

"Car?"

"No trace of it. We put out a BOLO and have been doing a rudimentary search along her route home, but so far nothing. Her family is having some Missing posters made up. Nobody who knows the girl believes she'd take off like this. She had lots of friends, was smart enough, but didn't want to go away to college. Father owns several appliance stores, and she was doing book-keeping for him."

"No blowups?"

"I haven't heard even a whisper that there was any-thing wrong." Drew's tone was downright grim.

Alan would have said no to just about anyone com-ing out here to ask anything of him, but this… Crap. He'd spent his entire adult life serving and protecting, in one way or another. Grimacing, he asked, "So what is it you think I can do for you?"

"Supervise a group of volunteers doing a search, to start. We plan to fan out every direction from the site of the party—which was in the woods, by the way. Couple of miles from here. If you held on to your dive gear, you might be able to investigate lakes or sink-holes in the area if it comes to that. You know we have a bunch of them, and some are deep."

The two of them had gone swimming in forbidden places, too, reckless as only kids that age could be. Then, he hadn't had the gear to explore flooded caves, but he'd wanted to.

Ignoring his reluctance to get involved, Alan nod-ded. "I can do that." His hand explored his jaw. "I might even shave so I don't scare anyone. Where do we meet?"

They would gather not two miles away, where a dirt road led into a dense stretch of woodland perfect for groups of teens to hide their activities from parents and patrolling sheriff's deputies.

"Thank you." Drew pushed himself to his feet, lines scoring his forehead. He started toward the front door but stopped. "You get out of the navy recently?"

"No, five years ago."

"Just out of curiosity, what have you been doing the past five years?"

Alan's mouth curved into a smile, rare for him these days, at the irony of all this. "I became a cop, what else?"

"THIS IS *SO* CREEPY!" one of Lucy's friends exclaimed—and she or one of the others had said more or less the same thing half a dozen times. Despite the early hour, they were all frenetic, Lucy most of all.

Lucy's melodrama might be normal for her age under the circumstances, but it unsettled Jo as it had since her sister made the big announcement yesterday. The sixteen-year-old was wired, as if she'd taken an upper. She was in constant motion, jittery, her voice edging into shrill.

On the other hand, well, her friends seemed to be acting the part of shock and horror as if they were auditioning in Hollywood.

Maybe I'm overthinking this, Jo thought, and made an effort to look around instead.

A good-sized crowd had showed up to search for Amy, which shouldn't be a surprise. This was a small enough town, people knew each other. A couple of clipboards with a headshot photo of Amy were being passed around. Seeing it a few minutes ago had made all this more frighteningly real.

A question nagged at the back of Jo's mind, though. Did walking the woods really make sense? People were saying that all the kids who'd been at the party agreed she'd left in her car. If, say, it had broken down and she'd had to get out and walk, where was the car? Could authorities have planned this search just to look as if they were doing something meaningful? Or did they have a reason to believe someone had lied?

Maybe cops *always* took into account the likelihood they'd been lied to.

Naturally, Amy was all anyone could talk about. In fact, right behind Jo now, a man said, "I hear no one else leaving the party drove the same way she did." He sounded knowledgeable, although who knew? What if one of the other partygoers had, in fact, left ahead of Amy and then waited beside the road until he saw her car?

"Where'd you hear that?" a woman asked, just as Jo turned to see who the guy was.

No one she recognized, but he replied, "Deputy Frazier told me when I asked."

"Oh."

Several people made shushing sounds.

Her gaze went to the three men standing together, apparently prepared to start organizing the milling group now that there were almost no new arrivals. Two were in uniform, both sheriff's deputies. One was a stranger to Jo, the other vaguely familiar. He'd been so far ahead of her in school she wouldn't have recognized him if she hadn't seen him a few times around town when she was home visiting. Brody had known who she was describing and said his name was Andrew Frazier. He was a good-looking guy with sandy hair and an athletic build. She'd passed him once coming out of the grocery store in town with a three- or four-year-old boy riding his shoulders, accompanying a woman who also looked familiar pushing a cart that held an even younger child.

The second deputy was shorter, chunky. Thick neck, square face. Obviously trying to appear authoritative, he had the shaved-head thing going she hated, and now stood with his feet braced apart and his hands resting on the wide leather belt, one really close to his holstered weapon. He had his eye on the guy who wasn't in uniform, and his expression verged on hostile.

Even if she weren't wondering what that was about, the third man was the one to command Jo's attention. Uniform or not, something about the way he carried himself said he was a cop, too. Tall, as much as six foot three or four, he would dominate any crowd with those broad shoulders and long, lean body. Not quite handsome, his face could better be described as craggy, with a strong jaw and chin, and a gaze that swept the crowd as if he expected gunfire to break out at any minute.

That gaze met hers as she watched him and paused. In fact, they stared at each other just a little too long considering they were strangers. From this distance she couldn't tell what color his eyes were, but felt an odd cramp inside before he continued to scan the faces of the volunteers.

Maybe their hands, too, she speculated. His expression wasn't trusting.

Who the heck was he?

Deputy Frazier spoke up then, overriding other voices. He introduced himself, Deputy Hudson and Alan Burke, who he said had a military and law enforcement background, without being specific.

Wait. The Burkes had owned the property neighboring the Summerlin land for as long as she could remember. Rod used to grumble about the piece of scum over there. Not this Alan, who was too young, but hadn't there been a son who lived somewhere else? If so, he'd made Rod mad over the years, too, by refusing to sell his place to her stepfather.

She tuned in to learn the group was being divided into four groups—a khaki-clad man had joined the other three. Apparently he was head of the local search and rescue group.

Without any such intention, Jo found herself under Alan Burke's authority. Brody had wandered away a few minutes ago to talk to friends and would be with Deputy Hudson. Lucy—Jo looked around. There she was, hanging back, but apparently joining yet a third group with several of her friends. She gave Jo one defiant look.

Rod hadn't been happy about his family ditching their duties at the cavern to join the search, insisting girls Amy's age were known for being unreliable, but after Jo had spoken up, had irritably conceded it might be the right thing to do. Austin was there, and Rod had called in two of the summer help who'd arrived this week, neither locals who would have known the missing woman, to keep tours going. He had full bookings today, so she understood. It was only fair to people who'd bought tickets in advance.

She was abruptly recalled to her purpose here when Burke spread a local topographical map open against a tree trunk and had everyone in his group study the area delineated by a red marker. A couple of people seemed to be having trouble making out landmarks, but most of them knew the area well enough to nod. He directed them to walk as far apart as they could without losing sight of the people on each side of them. His gaze moved from one face to the next.

"Call out to those folks if you need to leave the line to check out a heavy clump of shrubbery or a break in the land," he said, in a calm, deep voice. "We ended up with the most challenging terrain, including a rugged side slope. All we can do is our best. I see some of you brought walking sticks. They're good to use to poke around. Keep an eye out for snakes, especially those of you who aren't wearing boots."

Jo glanced around to see that some wore athletic shoes that left ankles exposed.

"The left side of our line will meet up with the river in half a mile or so."

Maybe a mile downriver from the Summerlin land, Jo calculated.

"That will keep us oriented," he continued. "There is a sinkhole here—" He tapped the almost round blue spot on the map. "We'll split to circle it. I want to know if anything catches your attention: a shoe or any other sign a person was here, some broken branches, scuffed ground, tire tracks. *Anything*. Got that?"

Heads bobbed, including Jo's. Riveting blue eyes compelled attention.

"I'll be at the uphill end because that's the hardest walking, and I have the experience. I'll also do some moving around to stay in contact with all of you. Okay?"

More nods.

Saying, "You, you, you," he got them in line. Jo was more than disconcerted to find herself directly to his left. Did he see her as a weak link he had to watch over? Or know somehow who she was and assume she must have done some hiking and scrambling in the area?

Theirs was the first of the four groups to start out. A married couple Jo knew vaguely had been positioned on one end; she could just make out their voices. Otherwise…she became aware of a heaviness in the air, the beginning of summer humidity, and a quiet that didn't seem quite natural. Birds and small animals had probably hunkered down at the sight of these humans intruding in a mostly deciduous forest that made it easy to imagine Indigenous hunters slipping from tree to tree. She could hear herself breathing, every rustle and crunch underfoot.

The guy to her left made more noise than seemed necessary. She had to keep turning her head to be sure Alan Burke was still there, though, so quietly did he move through the wooded landscape. It wasn't as if they had any reason to avoid making noise, she reminded herself. In fact…the hush here in the dappled light beneath the tangle of trees felt eerie today.

As if in response to her thought, a shriek made her heartbeat leap. She heard a sharp oath from the man to her right just before a flicker of bright blue settled her nerves. Blue jays did *not* like intruders in their woodlands.

Burke muttered, "I'd forgotten that sound."

"Shortened my lifespan," she mumbled.

A surprising, crooked grin told her he'd heard her.

His eyes were almost as bright a blue as the wings of the jay.

Twice he left his place in the line to take a look at something that caught someone's attention; both times he shook his head at the others as he returned.

She was sweating and scratched up by the time he called, "Spread the word down the line. We'll take a short break."

Jo spotted a newly downed tree and headed for it. The guy to the left gravitated the other direction, probably to join a friend. Alan Burke walked right to her and sat only a couple of feet away, stretching out his long legs.

"Hope everyone is up to the steep terrain."

"They all look fit." She hesitated. "I'm Jo Summerlin. I have a feeling we might be neighbors."

"Jo?"

"Short for Josephine." She took her water bottle out of the day pack she carried.

He did the same. "Ah. I keep hearing from a Rod Summerlin. He your father?"

"Stepfather."

Those sharp eyes watched her with more intensity than seemed natural. Was he hyperalert, or was it something about her?

"Rod is all about the cavern. He wants to own the whole thing."

"It might go on for miles," he pointed out. "Some of them do. The whole region may sit on top of a complicated interconnected labyrinth."

"But there's another opening on your land. At least… assuming you do live near us?"

He took a long drink of water without taking his gaze from her. "I'm one of those Burkes."

At his dry tone, she frowned, only vaguely recalling the talk about his father. Like he was the town drunk? Or…no, he manufactured and sold methamphetamine. That was it.

"I don't remember you from when I was a kid."

"I have to be older than you are," he said shortly. "I left to live with my grandparents before we'd likely have met in school."

She nodded. When he stayed silent, she asked, "Why this search? I mean, Amy left that party in a car, right?"

"So I'm told." His head tipped. "Do you know her?"

Thank goodness he hadn't said *did*, as if he believed Amy was dead.

"I babysat her and her sister sometimes. I hadn't seen her as an adult until, oh, two or three years ago. She and my brother were dating at the time."

"Your brother?"

"Brody? He volunteered today, too. He's with Deputy Hudson."

Alan seemed to mull that over. "They weren't still together?"

"No, it's been a while. A year or two? He might know who she's seeing now."

"I'll pass that on."

What did he mean by that?

"Wait. Are you suggesting *Brody* would be a suspect if Amy really was abducted or attacked?" *Murdered.* That's what she really meant.

Dark eyebrows rose. "I'm not the investigator. Whoever it is would likely want to talk to any of Ms. Kendall's…friends."

Guys Amy had been involved with. *And I just set Brody up for that*, Jo thought. Except…had she? Any of Amy's friends would know she and Brody had been an item at one time. There'd undoubtedly been other boys since.

Alan watched her while she fussed before he finally sighed, tucked his water bottle back in a pack that was more sizeable than hers, then rose to his feet with effortless grace. He put two fingers in his mouth and let out a piercing whistle. "Let's get moving!"

Rising herself, Jo studied the steep slope of exposed rock, stunted trees and tangled undergrowth ahead, then the woods stretching into the distance with a high canopy and deep shade. She pictured it in the middle of the night, when even a nearly full moon wouldn't have penetrated the darkness.

This woodland would have been prettier earlier in

the spring, with the redbud, pawpaw, serviceberry and dogwood trees in bloom. Now… Goose bumps rose on Jo's arms as she imagined Amy, terrified, running, stumbling, looking desperately for a place to hide, even as her pursuer gained on her.

She shuddered, aware that the man beside her had noticed. But, after a moment, he gave a brief nod and walked away.

Other volunteers she could see were spreading out in readiness to resume the search. She shouldn't hold them up, but… To Alan Burke's broad back, she asked, "Do you think we'll find Amy today? Out here?"

He stopped, turned, his expression enigmatic. Muscles flexed in his jaw. "No. I don't expect to find her."

With a lump in her throat, Jo wondered whether he meant today, in the grid they'd been assigned to search…or whether he didn't expect Amy to be found at all. Ever.

Chapter Three

An hour later, Alan had dropped down the hillside, speaking briefly to each of the volunteers to be sure no one was struggling, when a piercing scream rang out. This one was from a human throat.

He spun and scrambled at a near run uphill, having to catch himself with a hand to the ground a few times. Damn, that had to have been Jo Summerlin. Could he have been wrong? Had she been unlucky enough to stumble across the body of a young woman she knew?

The last guy before her position in line was staring up. Sweat dripped down his red face. "I think she's all right," he said uncertainly.

Alan ignored him. Even given his level of conditioning, his heart beat viciously against his chest wall by the time he finally saw her, on her hands and knees.

The sight shook him, although he didn't understand why any more than he understood why she'd riveted him earlier, at first sight. Yeah, she was a looker, but nothing like the women who swarmed SEALs in any bar near a base. Jo Summerlin wasn't so much voluptuous as delicate, despite an above-average height for a woman. Dark haired and dark-eyed, her slim hips and leggy, lithe body consistent with the fine bones. Athletic, he'd thought.

Now twigs had tangled in the long hair that was sagging from a formerly smooth ponytail. Blood beaded a scratch across one cheek, and others decorated her forearms. Like all of them, she was sweating, but she didn't look hurt.

He lowered himself to a crouch in front of her. "What is it?"

"Oh." She blew air upward in obvious, if futile, hopes of shifting sweaty strands of hair from her forehead. "I'm sorry about the scream. I...was startled."

"What—?" And then he saw it, too. In fact, if he hadn't been so focused on getting to her, he'd have already noticed a faint trail leading to a rock face—and the dark opening into a cave that would have been obscured by the vegetation around it if they hadn't happened right on it. Water trickled out of one side, enough to have turned the first tumble of rocks below the cave mouth slick. Earlier in the spring, that might have been a real stream.

"A bobcat burst out," Jo explained. "I think he must live here. He brushed right against me and took off."

"That would do it," he conceded. Bobcats were shy and seldom seen.

"I...noticed what looks like a trail."

"I see it. It's probably made by animals, you know."

"I do, but..."

He frowned. The cool air from the opening reached him, carrying the familiar musty, heavy smell, in this case tainted by notes of blood, if he wasn't mistaken. Again—probably that was thanks to the predator that lived here, but the only way to be sure was to take a look.

"Why here?" He was arguing as much with himself as with her. "Can you imagine carrying an unconscious woman up this hillside?"

"Have you seen a picture of her?"

"Face only."

"She's petite," Jo told him. "Five foot one, maybe? And slender. I'll bet she doesn't weigh over a hundred pounds."

That might make her particularly appealing as a target for abduction, he couldn't help thinking.

"Is there a road into the sinkhole?" Jo asked.

He turned, seeing a glint of water over the tops of the trees.

"If this track goes down to there…"

She was right. It would be doable. And hell, why was he dragging his feet? He'd been asked to ensure that every square foot of his area was examined, and that included this unappealing hole in the hillside. He had to check this out, whether he had brought the basic equipment with him or not, but he wasn't excited about it.

"I need to go in."

"Not alone," she said firmly.

"Have you done any caving?"

"Are you kidding? It's the family business."

He let his eyebrows climb. "This—" he jerked his head toward the opening that wasn't more than three feet high by three or four wide "—doesn't have much in common with a cavern that could stand in for a ballroom."

"I don't love wriggling through chokes," she admitted, with a dignity he had to admire, "but I've done some of it."

He sighed. *He* didn't love trying to rearrange his very bones to squirm through an extremely narrow passage. "Okay. We won't go far—we don't dare without equipment. If this is navigable, I'll probably have to come back later, but maybe we can tell right away if anyone who is two-legged has ever been in there." He rose to his feet. "At least we can take one basic precaution. I'll pass the word so people know why we've disappeared."

Jo IMMEDIATELY REGRETTED her offer—okay, *demand*—that she accompany him. She didn't even enjoy passages that meant she had to crawl, and thus far in her life had balked at anything that would have required her to squirm like a snake and chance getting stuck. The fact that this cave had likely never been explored, and that she and Alan might be the first people who'd ever stepped foot in it…

Well.

Chickening out wasn't an option, though. She pictured Amy Kendall, first as a silly girl, then a pretty almost adult, and her spine stiffened.

Alan rejoined her, setting down his pack and rummaging inside. She did the same with hers, and both produced gloves and flashlights.

His mouth quirked. "You're not completely surprised."

"Around here, dogs uncover cave openings every time they try to bury a bone. Highway crews find new ones. Like you said, there's a subterranean maze under us."

"Maybe your stepfather would like to buy this piece of property," Alan said drily.

She let herself grin. "Who knows?"

He studied her boots and heavy jeans with a critical eye, then slung a coil of rope around his shoulders. All right," he said. "Here we go."

"Maybe I should go first—"

"Let's just take a look inside before we make any decisions."

He had to duck while straddling a barrier of rocks to get through the opening. She followed his example, feeling a momentary rush of relief from the cooler air. Right before she gagged.

All caves she'd been in had the smell of a house that had been shut up for decades. She'd already gotten used to it anew in the time she'd been home, but this was way worse, almost putrid, probably because the space was so much tighter.

Plus, bones and some bloody shreds of an animal—a rabbit, she thought queasily—gave evidence of the bobcat's residence. Now Jo was able to stand upright, but Alan had to stoop. One side of the cave gleamed wet, the wall glittery calcite. The single passage immediately narrowed again.

Alan frowned at it. "I wish we had helmets."

She didn't comment, and a moment later he seemed to shake himself. "Ladies first." That still-frowning gaze met hers. "Anything looks unstable, you stop."

What could she do but nod? It made sense that with his greater strength he follow her. He'd be a lot more capable of pulling her out of a bind, if it came to that, than she would be of dragging his much larger body so much as an inch or two.

She didn't have to squirm—forearms and knees were fine, and her shoulders and hips didn't touch the sides of the passage, but the knees of her jeans got wet right away, and icy water seeped inside her glove. The beam of her flashlight speared the darkness ahead, revealing nothing but a curve and…something that scuttled.

Ugh. A salamander, one of the cave denizens that also spent time outside. Harmless, and she didn't mind them, but thank goodness she hadn't set a hand down on it. She might have embarrassed herself by screaming again.

Within what she guessed was five minutes—although when crawling through the darkness, time began to feel less definite—she started to shiver. The caves in the Ozark region stayed at an average sixty degrees, which made them a temperate retreat for bats and bears and sundry other creatures that hibernated in Missouri's cold winters. For a woman who'd been sweating copiously, sixty degrees was chilly. Never mind the cold water.

A low voice came from behind her. "You okay?"

"Sure. Am I too slow? Sorry."

"No. It's more important to be careful than fast."

Given the bruises she could already feel forming on her knees and forearms from the rough floor of the cave—oh, what she'd give for pads—he was right. She peeked behind to see that his flashlight wasn't on. Smart. They shouldn't waste battery life in case… What? They got trapped in here?

This chill wasn't the same kind, because cave-ins did happen.

People knew where they were, Jo reminded herself, and went back to trying *not* to think about the weight of the earth above them, or the increasingly musty smell, or the fact that she felt as if the air had a weight, too. She hadn't seen any evidence that bats did occupy this cave, but their guano could poison the air.

Thank goodness she could hear the quiet sounds of Alan moving behind her. She wouldn't want to be alone.

Her beam of light was suddenly being swallowed by darkness. She stopped, sweeping the flashlight from side to side. The smaller passage had opened into a room. A good-sized one, she decided, before crawling forward a few more feet and standing. She turned to light the way for Alan, who rose to his feet, too, and switched on his own flashlight to examine a shining cavernous space with stalactites and stalagmites formed by the slow drip of calcite-rich water. These weren't eye-catching like the ones in Summerlin Cavern, but formed in the same crucible.

Here, the water seeped down the walls on all sides, and raking the ceiling with light, she saw wet cracks.

The cave went on, narrowing again, but wide enough Alan took a turn at going first. If they'd been walking, she would probably have been stepping on his heels, so close did she follow. They reached other rooms, beautiful but not spectacular, none showing signs of occupancy by anything but a few salamanders. The constantly seeping water wasn't deep enough for the crayfish that made their lives in the dark streams and pools of some caverns.

She was once again ahead, on her knees and forearms, when she heard a cracking sound. She'd barely begun to hunch, the words "Watch out!" stuck in her throat when something banged into the side of her head and her shoulder. She dropped flat on her belly.

"Jo! Damn it, I knew better! Are you all right?"

At his demand in that gritty voice, she cautiously lifted a hand to her head. With the gloves on, she couldn't tell if she was bleeding, or even if a lump was forming.

"Yes. I don't think it was that big a rock."

"We need to back out. Slowly, carefully. I'll move a foot or two, you move a foot or two. Try not to come in contact with either wall."

"Okay." She worked at regulating her breathing. "I need to get back up on my knees, though."

"I know you do."

His tone of gentle reassurance gave her the confidence to push back up. Resting back on her knees and forearms, her hand came down on a rock she didn't think had been there. She groped it. It was…oh, maybe the size of a baseball or a little bigger. A softball. It hadn't dropped all that far, or she could really have been hurt.

Quiet sounds came from behind her, then a hand closed on her ankle. "Your turn."

That first minute or two of their slow retreat was the most hair-raising. Once a section of the roof began to crack, at least a partial collapse could happen anytime.

They kept squirming backward, Alan murmuring things like, "That's good. Now hold up for a minute."

Then, suddenly, he said, "This space is big enough to sit up and take a rest. We can turn around."

Once she'd gotten up onto her butt, relief left her feeling momentarily weak. "Well, that was fun."

"I should have come back, not brought you in here to do a half-assed exploration with neither of us adequately prepared."

She reached out and closed her hand on his forearm. "A rock grazed me, that's all. If the whole roof had collapsed, you'd have dug me out."

He muttered something probably not meant for her ears before saying, "You're okay to keep going?"

"No problem." She'd have a bruise on her shoulder, she could already tell, and probably a modest lump on her head, not for the first time in her life. She'd hit her head a lot harder when she was learning to ride her bike in the cavern parking lot.

"We've been on our way longer than I meant anyway. Stick close to me."

Turning her head, she saw his face, eerily shadowed by the narrow beams of their flashlights. She guessed she looked owlish instead of mysterious.

"I don't know why anyone would have gone on," she agreed.

"I would have as a kid sure I'd find Spanish gold or pre-Columbian artifacts just a little farther along." Was that a smile in his voice?

"Lose your optimism?" Jo asked.

He was quiet just long enough to make her curious. Then, expressionless, he said, "You could say that."

Subject closed.

Making their way back toward the entrance felt torturously slow, despite the fact that they no longer had to exercise the same caution. She definitely had a headache now and was shivering besides. Plus, she felt the effects of the scrambling that had brought them to the cave opening in the first place. She tried to stay in shape during the school year, but jogging or using the elliptical didn't necessarily translate well to hiking along a rocky side hill.

Jo suppressed a whimper at the sight of daylight, and took pride in her stoicism as she crawled over the rough rocks at the entrance and out into the heat that immediately made her feel as if she'd immersed herself in a steam bath.

Alan looked so much the same as he had before they ventured into the earth, she felt disgruntled. His gaze was keen on her face, but she didn't meet his eyes until he said, "Let me take a look."

Wonderful. She tipped her head and felt his fingers sifting through her hair until he found what was definitely a bump. The bump, she discovered, wasn't the only part of her scalp that was oversensitized beneath his fingertips.

"You're bleeding a little." He didn't sound happy about it. "Okay, rotate your shoulder for me."

When she obliged to his satisfaction, he didn't make her bare her upper body, thank heavens. She had to wonder how bad she looked but didn't want to admit why that mattered.

"Did the others go on?" she thought to ask for the first time.

He grunted agreement. "I told them we'll hold to the same elevation and meet up with them at the sinkhole. Let's take a minute and have a bite to eat."

Jo nodded sturdily, put her flashlight and leather gloves in her day pack, and took out both a bottle of water and a bag of peanuts.

Alan sat down, stretched out those long, muscular legs clad in cargo pants and produced nuts and raisins from his pack.

He seemed disinclined to chat. As much as she'd have liked to ask him what he knew that volunteers like her didn't, she accepted his cue and didn't say a word.

KNOWING A ROCK had fallen onto Jo had given Alan a major scare. He hadn't known how big the damn thing was, whether the ceiling was about to cave in, whether she was unconscious, bleeding, hurt in some way that was *his* responsibility. They'd skated, but he wouldn't soon forget how narrow a miss they'd had even if he also knew he was blowing out of proportion what had been a minor incident. If she'd really been hurt— All he knew was, having *her* the one who'd been injured really ate at him. He'd clamped his mouth shut after checking her out, but those frightening moments kept running on an endless reel in his head.

This had to be an echo of the last disastrous police operation during which two hostages had been killed. Not his fault, but he never entirely let himself off the hook.

The search had otherwise been as pointless as Alan had expected. Didn't mean they wouldn't keep looking, although deciding where next had just become more difficult.

After the discovery of the cave, he'd started looking upslope and down with a different eye. How many other entrances were disguised by rocks or dense vegetation? But that speculation was easily confounded by the same logic that had made him hesitant to enter the cave they'd already penetrated. No woman on the run would climb up here. And why would a man who'd abducted a woman carry or force her this distance from any road? There had to be plenty of vacant houses and cabins in the area. His own house, plenty isolated, had been empty for enough years, it would have made an ideal site to hold a captive.

And, damn it, when looked at objectively, the odds still were that Amy Kendall had taken off on her own. It happened. Parents and friends didn't always know what was going through someone's head. Maybe she'd gotten on drugs, met a love interest she knew her parents would hate. Or she just wanted to become a free spirit.

Alan didn't believe any of that, not given the disap-
pearances of the other young women in this corner of
the state. All in their early twenties, all described as
beautiful. Four years ago, in Newton County, a young
woman named Christy Dodswell had been driving
home after babysitting her nieces and nephew. Neither
she nor her car had ever been found. Six months after
that, another young woman up in Lawrence County
had set out to walk home from a friend's house at one
in the morning and never arrived. A couple of years
back, Jeannie Kennedy had finished finals at the university in Springfield and decided to surprise her family by starting for home in the late afternoon instead
of waiting for morning. She'd made it partway, stopping at a tavern in an apparent impulse to celebrate her
twenty-first birthday. Her locked car was left barely
over a mile from her house. The fact that her luggage
and purse were missing along with the young woman
created speculation that she'd gone away with a man,
deliberately leaving behind the car that belonged to
her parents.

Because the sheriff's department lead detective was
refusing to believe the missing women could possibly be linked, or had been abducted rather than taking off on their own, Drew was the one who put in
calls to jurisdictions in neighboring states to find out
if there was any chance a predator had taken yet more
young women than the ones of which they were already
aware. It was a miracle that the sheriff had given him
the go-ahead.

Alan's gut said they'd eventually find more victims,

including runaways or prostitutes no one missed. Or women merely passing through the area who happened to catch a killer's eye when they stopped for gas or lunch at the wrong time and place. When they didn't arrive at their destinations, there was no reason anyone would suspect their journeys might have come to abrupt ends in a rural corner of Missouri.

After his group had reached the sinkhole and worked their way carefully around it—they found that, indeed, a track led up to a wide dirt area where cars could be parked, and that not all the people who swam here had picked up their trash before leaving.

He climbed up on a rock and looked down into water he suspected was very deep. He couldn't swear this was one he and Drew had dove into but had a suspicion it was. It sure as hell would be a good place to make a body vanish, were it tied to a concrete block or the like.

"Climbing back up here after a swim wouldn't be easy," a soft voice said from beside him.

He started. Jo Summerlin, of course. Maybe his radar had dismissed her as a threat. He couldn't imagine how else he had failed to hear her approach.

"That's part of the fun."

"You'd dive off here?"

His shoulders moved. "Probably have. Ten years old, I thought I was capable of anything." Except, on some level, he'd known that wasn't true. He couldn't keep his father from battering his mother or him, or her from growing less and less present, physically and in every other way, once she too became addicted to the methamphetamine that was the livelihood and curse of Alan's father.

Too bad it hadn't killed him sooner, Alan thought now, almost dispassionately.

He shook off dark memories, aware of Jo watching him. He still hadn't quite figured out why the sight of her had hit him so hard, but he would have been smart to position her somewhere else down the line of searchers instead of near enough for him to keep an eye on her all day.

What he'd learned was that she was fit, graceful, more observant than he liked, brave and able to laugh at herself. He wasn't likely to see much if anything of her after today, though, and told himself that would be best. He was in no state to start something with a woman, and particularly one as normal as her. She'd come home for the summer to be with her family, a concept that was alien to him.

Still, he was curious about her. "You grew up here. Didn't you let yourself get a little wild sometimes?"

She made a sound that might have been meant to be a laugh, and he'd swear her eyes had darkened. "No." She spoke even more softly. "I…didn't really have the chance."

Because she'd had parents who gave a damn about her?

"What do you do for a living?" he asked.

"I'm a teacher. This past year I had second graders, and will again come fall."

An elementary school teacher. Of course she was.

Not for him, even if he'd been so inclined. Which he wasn't.

"I think I hear our ride coming," he said, and she nodded.

He had absolutely no idea what she was thinking.

Chapter Four

"The missing woman is all the tourists could talk about." Rod shook his head as he scanned the serving dishes filling the center of the table.

Surprised, Jo paused with her fork halfway to her mouth. "How did they hear about her?"

"Town." He shrugged, stabbing what was at least a third slice of meatloaf from the platter and transferring it to his plate. "Cafés, grocery store, bed-and-breakfast, the lodge."

That made sense. Mayville *was* a small town. Dramatic events like this didn't happen often.

"You'd have said if they found anything." That was Rod again, not even really asking a question. Of course they would have.

"We didn't," Brody said tightly. He'd been withdrawn since coming home.

"It was boring." Lucy bit her lip. "I mean, it was scary, too. I kept thinking—" She broke off.

Jo nodded. "I was as afraid of finding her as I was of not."

Lucy looked grateful. "Yeah."

Brody frowned at Jo. "You got stuck with that Burke guy."

Rod's head came up. "Burke? The neighbor?"

"Yes, Alan Burke," Jo agreed. "Have you met him?"

"I didn't even know he was in town. I've written him half a dozen times." He mumbled something she felt sure was less than complimentary. "What the hell is he doing back here?"

"I don't know. We didn't get personal." They were all staring at her. Jo hesitated, then said, "We came across a cave on that steep hillside south of the highway. A bobcat burst out of it, scaring the daylights out of me."

"A cave?" Rod and Brody echoed in unison.

Two of a kind.

"Nothing that interesting. I went into it with Alan, because I didn't think he should go alone. It was obviously the bobcat's den. It stunk." Her audience didn't care about that. "We followed it for a ways, mostly on hands and knees, found a few rooms but nothing very interesting. I wondered it if might connect to our cavern."

Rod leaned forward. "Where was it exactly?"

She did her best to pinpoint the location for him, wondering if he planned to check it out. If so, he didn't say so.

Once satisfied, Rod asked, "They done with this search nonsense?"

"It's *not* nonsense!" Lucy cried. "Amy has to be *somewhere*."

Rod snorted. "Probably Kansas City or Des Moines

by now. I still don't understand why the sheriff's department jumped the gun like this. Girls that age are undependable. We all know that. Her car is missing, right? Where do they think *it* is? Something probably happened at that party. Her boyfriend broke up with her, maybe, and she took off."

Jo raised her eyebrows. Boys were solid as the earth, girls undependable? She didn't think so. "From what I hear," she said, after giving Lucy a tiny shake of her head, "Amy is levelheaded. No one believes she's the kind to get so dramatic, or to scare her parents this way. If she was abducted, the man who did it could have taken her car someplace. Left it in an abandoned barn." She decided not to share the thought she'd had today about the seemingly bottomless depths of the sinkhole people with a lot more courage than she had apparently swam in.

Rod tightened his jaw, evidently realizing he had just been chided, but all he said was a curt, "So what's the plan for tomorrow?"

"As far as I know, no mass searches." Jo looked at her siblings.

"That's what Deputy Hudson told us," Brody agreed. "He seemed to think the whole thing was a waste of time. But *he* didn't know Amy."

"Was she dating anyone recently?" Jo asked.

Brody looked down at his now-cleared plate. "I don't know. I didn't see her very often and we didn't really talk."

Disturbed, Jo wondered if he was lying. Or was it only that he wished Amy Kendall *had* been talking to him? What had broken the two of them up? Just that Brody had gone off to college and Amy felt left behind? That might explain him blaming Jo for him having "wasted" his time these past two years.

The atmosphere subdued, they all finished eating. Whatever their worries, the two men dug into big slices of apple pie topped with ice cream, while Lucy and Jo declined it.

Jo had just opened the dishwasher when, out of the corner of her eye, she saw Lucy sidling toward the hall and the foot of the staircase.

"Stop right there. You're not leaving me with this."

"Why can't Brody help?" her sister asked sulkily.

"He doesn't know it yet, but tomorrow it's his turn. I'm setting up a schedule." Foolishly, she'd assumed that once Lucy and Brody were old enough Rod would have made Brody help in the kitchen, too. Apparently not. Jo wasn't about to put up with that, not when she and Lucy worked just as hard all day at the cavern. Brody had grumbled at her insistence but fallen in line. Rod hadn't said a word. "I don't mind doing a lot of the cooking this summer," she added now, "but the least you can do is help with the cleanup."

"Oh, fine." Lucy stomped back into the dining room, returning a minute later with several nearly empty serving dishes.

Jo started rinsing dishes before putting them in the dishwasher. "Are you as tired as I am?"

"I don't know. Where we were was mostly flat. You really found a new cave?"

"Like that's news around here?"

For once, the teenager grinned. "I guess not. But…a bobcat?"

"It actually brushed against my leg. I just about had a heart attack."

Lucy giggled. "I know I would have." She sneaked a sidelong look at Jo. "He's kind of hot. That Burke guy."

Jo made a face. "Yes, he is hot. Closemouthed, though." More than that: grim was a better description. Her heart gave a peculiar jump when she remembered the one grin. "I don't know anything about him. Do you?"

Lucy grabbed a pan out of the dish drainer and started to dry it. "Only that he's living out there. The house has been empty for *years*. Someone said he's been in the navy."

Military. Deputy Frazier had said so, but Jo would have guessed just from the way he carried himself and the air of command that appeared to be part of him.

"Do you know why Rod wants that property so bad?" Jo asked.

A shaken head. "Except… Dad is all about the cavern. Like that's news. Maybe he's afraid someone will widen that opening and start competing with him. That would have to hurt business."

"I didn't think of that." Jo paused momentarily, shook her head and put the last dinner plate into the dishwasher. "I don't remember that end of the cave being spectacular enough to make him jealous."

"You've been in it?"

"Years ago with Dad and Brody." Curious, she

asked, "You know that Brody wants to extend the tours into other passages?"

"Sure." Lucy jerked one shoulder. "Why not? There are other cool rooms out there."

"Rod never seemed interested in expanding, unless that's why he wants to buy the Burke land."

Lucy slipped the damp dish towel through the handle of the refrigerator. "You remember how he used to keep the keys to the gates hanging right inside his office?"

"Sure." Worried, she studied her sister's fine-boned face.

"Brody and I used them a few times, like, the past couple of years."

"You mean, you went exploring?" The idea quickened her pulse. Brody might have the common sense to equip himself for safety and bring along an experienced friend or two, but Lucy had been displaying too much impulsive behavior this summer to make Jo think she'd have done the same.

"I guess Brody did." A purely malicious expression crossed the girl's face. "He had parties back in there a few times, too, when Dad was gone."

"Parties." Inebriated teenagers wandering unfettered in parts of the cavern that were still in their "wild" state. Had they damaged delicate formations? What if there was a shaft somewhere? One wrong step, and a kid could stumble over the edge to his death.

"It was fun!" Lucy said defiantly. "When I saw people leaving and he told me what they'd done, I had one, too!"

Aghast, Jo exclaimed, "You *know* how dangerous that could be."

With an exaggerated shrug, Lucy backed away. Hot color touched her cheekbones, and her jaw was set. "Nobody got hurt. But I had to tell Dad because— It doesn't matter. Now he's hidden the keys. I can't find them anywhere."

Jo appraised her sister, sensing something feverish simmering just below the surface. "Why would you want to?" she asked, going for calm.

"Because…because…" Tears formed in her eyes. "Jesse Phipps found something." She gasped. "I don't know why I'm bothering! You wouldn't believe me, either." Naturally, she turned and bolted.

Jo heard running footsteps on the stairs before she could decide to pursue.

Brody had left immediately after dinner. Jo had no idea whether he had a girlfriend, or what. Lucy stayed closeted in her room. Jo waited a good fifteen minutes to make sure her sister didn't plan to reappear, then rapped her knuckles on the half-open door of her stepfather's office.

"Jo?" He looked away from his computer monitor, peering over a pair of glasses he'd started needing in the past couple of years. "What's up?"

She went in and sat down in the extra chair beside his desk. "Lucy told me something."

An expression of resignation crossed his face. "About the skull."

"The *what*?"

His eyebrows rose. "She didn't tell you."

"She said a friend of hers found 'something.'"

Rod grimaced. "That would be it. Did she admit that she and her brother both threw some wild parties deep in the cavern?"

Jo nodded. "Although she didn't say wild."

"What do you think?"

Of course a bunch of teenagers had been drunk, if not using illegal substances.

Seeing her expression, he grunted. "Just imagine the appeal. Pitch-dark except for a few flashlights, the drip of water, strange formations and shadows, weird echoes. What could be better?"

"Did they do any damage?"

"In a few places. I gave 'em hell, which neither of them appreciated," he growled. "I still can't believe they were so careless with a precious natural resource that's our livelihood, on top of everything else!"

"I didn't know you were ever away from home long enough at night for them to do something like that—" She broke off. It wasn't her business where he'd been.

But he said, "Seeing a woman. Thought Lucy and Brody were old enough to be responsible when I was gone for a few hours, or even overnight."

Jo could only bob her head. She'd have thought the same. She also wondered if he'd been "seeing a woman" when she was growing up, too. She'd always assumed his absences in the evening meant he'd gone back to the cavern offices to work. As if that kind of history mattered now.

Chagrined, she said, "I'm not getting anywhere with Lucy. Maybe I'm too much of a mother figure for her."

"Give her time." He sighed and settled deeper into his chair. "She seemed fine early in the fall. I'm not even sure when this hysteria set in."

"When her friend claimed to see bones?"

Her stepfather spread his hands in frustration. "Why would that stir her hormones? For God's sake, I listened! I went so far as to call a sheriff's deputy out to join me and led him to where that kid claimed he'd seen a skull, but we couldn't find a damn thing!" He blew out a breath. "Wish we had. Just think of the publicity if we'd found the skeleton of a nineteenth-century train robber. Better yet, complete with a chest full of gold."

Jo laughed. "We could rewrite the tour narrative."

He grinned, making her feel as if he was relating to her as an adult rather than the kid she'd been. In too many of her memories, he'd been stressed, demanding or flat-out dismissive with his family, in painful contrast to his charm with the tourists. Now he sighed again. "The kids were drunk, that's all, crashing around where they didn't belong, and spooked themselves."

"So now you're hiding the keys to the gates?"

"Damn straight I am! Do you blame me?"

"No," she admitted. "That was…really dumb of them. I'm especially surprised at Brody risking any damage to the cavern."

"He can't seem to understand that his brainstorm about extended tours would do damage, too. I figure as it is, we're protecting huge parts of the cavern while providing access to spectacular rooms and formations.

That's enough to give people a good idea of the wonders deep inside the earth."

His argument made sense, Jo couldn't help thinking, sympathetic as she was to Brody's desire to do something more exciting while setting his own stamp on the management of the Summerlin Cavern.

"You think they'd do the same thing if you gave them access again?"

Lines darkened his expression. "I'm hoping not Brody. God knows with Lucy. I can't rely on her at all anymore."

"I can see that."

"Everything is high drama. This thing with the missing young woman. You'd think she'd been Lucy's best friend."

Jo squeezed her fingers together. Tentatively, she suggested, "Maybe it has to do with Mom leaving us the way she did. Just…never coming back. It could be a sore place that Lucy's never acknowledged."

His gaze sharpened. "You took it in stride. Your mother didn't have what it took to stick it out, and you knew it. Young as Lucy was, why would she have missed her?"

He had no clue how hard her mother abandoning her *had* hit her. She still bore the bruises. But Jo said only, "She was two. Well, almost three. Psychologists think a lot that impacts our psyche is introduced by that age."

Rod snorted. He wasn't the most sensitive of men, which probably had something to do with his divorce from Jo's mother, who always cried when movies ended on a sad note. "All I can say is, she better get over it.

Summer is when we make most of our income. She needs to get her act in gear. I'm not going to put up with much more of this nonsense."

"It would help if Amy Kendall was found," Jo said, but knew immediately she was wrong. If Amy Kendall was found dead, which seemed increasingly likely whatever Rod said to the contrary, Lucy wasn't the only member of this family who would be traumatized. The whole community would be shaken.

Her stepfather didn't say a word, which made her wonder if he wasn't thinking the same thing. Unless his intense focus on his cavern and family left him entirely indifferent to Amy's fate.

UNOFFICIALLY, ALAN JOINED the next stage of the search, too. The department was too thinly staffed to allow deputies to use much time driving every road and turn up every dirt track, never mind looking inside every derelict structure in the county. Some were volunteering their days off, as was one officer from the Mayville PD, but that was still a drop in the bucket. Alan had no deadline for restoring the house or selling it; truth be told, he didn't mind having a purpose again. A mission, of sorts. His willingness made him wonder if he hadn't turned a corner from the zombie he'd been after walking away from his job and the police department, his ability to believe in his fellow officers broken into rubble. He still had no idea what he could do next with his life.

Today, out of curiosity he took the road leading to

the Summerlin Cavern. He hadn't seen more than the billboard out on the highway since he was a kid.

The approach was beautiful, all gray rocks and vivid spring growth, the plunge down to the river. Even the parking lot didn't detract much from the setting. The giant half-moon of the cavern opening would inspire awe and primal uneasiness in almost anybody.

The parking lot was mostly full, some animated people walking back from the gray stone building toward the cars, most carrying bags that presumably held souvenirs bought at the gift shop. A road marked No Trespassing continued around a curve out of sight.

Still driven by curiosity, Alan parked in the lot, then walked down that narrow road. A hundred yards, and there was a two-story farm-style house, a detached garage and little room for anything you could call a yard.

A dog started barking inside the house. Alan could see him through the front window. Homely animal, but he knew his job.

What Alan hadn't expected was the front door to open. A woman appeared, gripping the dog's collar. Jo-for-Josephine Summerlin herself.

Only then did Alan acknowledge that he hadn't been curious about the cavern; he'd speculated about Jo. Wanted to see where she'd grown up, to know whether she was home only for a brief visit or for the summer.

"Alan?" she said, surprise in her voice.

No avoiding this now. He shouldn't have let himself get drawn here in the first place. "Jo. Just being nosy. I haven't been over here since I was nine or ten years old."

"Rusty won't bite," she promised, and released the dog. Still barking, the mutt raced toward him, circled him a couple of times, then succumbed to the lure of an outstretched hand. Fingernails down his back erased his caution and he happily accompanied Alan toward the front porch.

"Would you like some lemonade?" Jo asked, gesturing toward a row of comfortable-looking Adirondack chairs on the broad porch.

Thank you, no. I shouldn't be here.

His mouth opened and he heard himself saying, "Thanks."

She smiled and disappeared inside. Alan went to one end of the porch and peered down at a stretch of river, water tumbling over rocks. Even at a season when the water was high, there wasn't enough channel for boating of any kind, not on this stretch. A dock, probably built for fishing or just dangling feet in the cold water, stretched out from the rocky bank.

When he heard the screen door squeak behind him, he went back to the chairs and sat in one. She set a tray down with a pitcher and two glasses on a small table. Then they gazed at each other.

He was uncomfortably reminded of his first sight of her when the volunteers gathered for the search. He'd had trouble tearing his gaze from her, even though at the time he'd had no idea why.

He still didn't, not entirely.

"Can you tell me what's happening with the search?" she asked, breaking the too-long silence.

He saw no reason not to share what he knew. Her forehead crinkled at his explanation.

"Is that why you're *here*?"

"No. I might have driven as far as the parking lot and turned around, just to be sure there were no driveways off your road, but I remembered that much. You're clinging to the hillside here."

"No kidding," she said wryly. "Lucky no one in this house sleepwalks."

He laughed, something he hadn't done much of in a while. She seemed to have that effect on him.

"Rusty likes you," she observed.

Alan had hardly noticed that the dog had rested its head on his thigh, and he'd been petting him. Now he scratched the itchy area under the collar. "I've always liked dogs."

"You don't have one?"

He shook his head. "We had a dog when I lived with my grandparents. Since then…" He shrugged. "I was active duty military, then a cop. Not home enough."

Darker striations showed in eyes that were a chocolate brown in the slanting sunlight. "Someone told me you were navy, but not the cop part. No wonder they roped you in for the search."

"Drew Frazier and I were friends as kids." He glanced at her. "Deputy Frazier. He's the one who thought I could help." He kept waiting for her to ask why he was here, but apparently it hadn't occurred to her that he might have reason to stop by that was unrelated to the search. Instead she asked if anybody had found anything.

"Not that I've heard." He took a long drink of lemonade.

"If her car isn't found—" She sounded more strained than he'd expect, given that she wasn't close to the missing young woman. "Will authorities just give up?"

"They'll be talking to everyone who was at the party or friends of Ms. Kendall, here and from college. Try to get a look at her social media accounts, in case she's been in contact with anyone unexpected or hints at a plan she hasn't confided in her local friends about."

Suddenly wary, she said, "Nobody has talked to Brody yet, as far as I know."

"Sheriff's department's single detective isn't convinced police should be involved yet. Even when—if—he gets there, he's one man. Lot of people to talk to."

Jo bit her lip and nodded. She hadn't so much as sipped her lemonade. Instead, her fingers were twined tightly together on her lap.

Not taking his eyes from her, he said, "There comes a time when there won't be anything more the department can do."

She swallowed. "I…understand."

Did she really? He couldn't help speculating on the tension he'd felt in her from their first meeting. Could she suspect her brother? Knew about a recent argument, maybe?

The cop in him had to press. "This Amy isn't related to you or a friend of yours. You seem…more upset than I'd expect." And, damn, his tone sounded clinical.

He got what he deserved. A flash of shock, supplanted by anger. She shot to her feet. "I don't even want to think about what you're suggesting, Mr. Burke. Excuse me, I'm expected at the gift shop."

What could he do but rise, too? He didn't wait for her to take the lemonade to the kitchen so they could walk together. He was pretty sure he'd just burned any bridge they'd formed between them yesterday, which was probably just as well. Keeping his distance from her would be smart.

Chapter Five

The visit from Alan Burke lingered in Jo's mind as the day dragged on. Why *had* he stopped by, and gone to the trouble of walking as far as the house? He never had said. *My fault*, she acknowledged.

She asked her brother and sister, casually, if he'd also stuck his head into the gift shop. Both had looked surprised.

"Not that I saw," they said in unison.

Did Brody look apprehensive?

Since Alan couldn't possibly consider her, Jo, a suspect, she had to wonder if his goal had been sounding her out about her family. Because that's what he'd done, wasn't it? And if *that* was so, he had to be more involved in the investigation than he'd admitted. Had he been a detective when he was a cop?

How dumb had she been to let her guard down with him. He was an attractive man. Fine, but her loyalty was to her family.

In the midst of straightening a display of T-shirts, she looked down to see that her hands had gone still.

Silly. The investigation didn't have anything to do with her family!

Except…she'd imagined Brody looked evasive a couple of times. And then there was the fact that he'd been seriously into Amy, and never said what had broken them up.

Except, that wasn't all. It was Lucy, too. Something had her scared, and Jo had to wonder if it wasn't fear for her brother.

Jo brooded about it for the rest of the day, then followed Lucy up to her bedroom and slipped inside before her sister could slam the door in her face.

The pretty teenager backed up until she bumped into her bed. "This is *my* room! What are you doing here?"

Jo leveled a look at her. "I want to hear what this friend of yours found in the cavern, and why you're so sure I won't believe you. Have I ever let you down?"

"You aren't here enough to do that," her sister retorted.

She'd known right where to slip the blade between Jo's ribs. Everything Jo had tormented herself with was true, then; Lucy did believe her big sister had abandoned her, just as their mother had abandoned them both. Despite the pain, Jo was determined not to let herself get paralyzed by guilt. She *hadn't* abandoned Lucy; she'd been a good big sister. If she should have done more, well…she couldn't go back, but she could help untangle whatever it was that tormented Lucy *now*.

"Dad said your friend—Jesse?—found a skull."

Lucy sagged into a sitting position on the edge of

the bed, looking defeated. She crossed her arms as if trying to hug herself. "*He* didn't believe us."

"Us?" Jo edged toward the bed. "Did you see it, too?"

"No, but Jesse started to yell and he came running out of the dark like he'd seen a ghost or something. He was really freaked."

Jo sat down beside the teenager. "Did he have a flashlight with him?"

Lucy nodded. "Everyone did."

One smart decision.

"Didn't anyone go back with him to look?"

She shook her head. "*Everyone* was freaked. You know? I mean, that was part of the fun, but Jesse went off by himself and it was really dark, and even *I* don't know that part of the cavern very well. I should have gone, but—"

She, too, had been scared. And was now ashamed because she hadn't been brave enough to find out whether her friend had told the truth.

"You didn't go very far up any of the passages, did you? I mean, for the party?"

"No, just that room with the shallow pool. You know the one?"

Jo did.

"It's big, and there aren't a lot of stalagmites or stalactites that anyone could damage, and I didn't tell anyone the water isn't really deep, even though it looks like it is. If they stumbled in, they couldn't drown." More common sense. "I didn't think anyone would want to go off by themselves, because the passage gets really narrow after that."

It did. Claustrophobically so. That was one reason the section of the cavern had never been included in tours. It *could* be; the stretch where Jo always felt as if she needed to suck in her stomach to make herself skinny only extended five or ten feet. It could be part of the thrill to the wild tour that Brody was envisioning.

"You told Dad where Jesse saw the skull?"

"Of course I did!" Lucy's eyes were as dark as Jo's, and right now they were huge. "He *said* he searched, but—"

"Why don't you believe him?" Jo asked, puzzled.

"I guess 'cuz he was mostly mad about us using the cavern for drunken parties," she mumbled. "That's what he called them, even though we didn't have *that* much to drink. I could *tell* he didn't really believe me."

Jo had no trouble imagining why he'd been doubtful, assuming that was the case. Young teens having fun getting wasted and scaring themselves silly were likely to have wild imaginations. Say, seeing a round rock shadowed with indentations that could be eye sockets in a brief flare of a flashlight. Not that she'd say as much to Lucy.

"He says he did go back there. He even had a deputy with him. He told me he wishes they had found a skeleton. Like a long-ago train robber."

Lucy let out a watery giggle. "I bet he would like that."

They sat for a minute in silence. Lucy broke it.

"Yesterday, did you really go in a cave nobody had ever explored? Weren't you scared?"

"Not really." Jo smiled. "I had a big, brawny man right behind me. I knew he could pull me out of trouble, no problem."

Lucy giggled again.

Jo frowned. "Is this Jesse especially brave? Was he trying to show off for you or another girl?"

"Show off? Nuh-uh. He's really scrawny, so he fit through the passage without it being a big deal."

"Did he say why he wandered off?"

"Yeah, he heard strange sounds and then Rusty barking—" Expression apprehensive, Lucy grabbed Jo's hand. "I didn't tell Dad Rusty was with us. You won't tell him, will you? He'd be even madder."

Jo hesitated. It wasn't uncommon to hear eerie moans or rattles or other weird sounds. The wind and water moved through cracks, and earth settled. Occasionally, a rock broke off.

The dog's presence, though…that increased the likelihood of Lucy's story being true. Rusty could have smelled human remains, even really old ones. He might have picked something up and brought it partway back, then barked out of excitement. Or just because he enjoyed the echo. Only—would he have carried the skull away again, dropping it who knew where before he heard Lucy calling for him?

On a shiver, Jo thought, *maybe*.

"I won't tell Dad," she said after a moment.

But apprehension prickled over her skin as she remembered how worked up Rusty had been the night Amy Kendall disappeared. The two things couldn't possibly have anything to do with each other…but the

dog hadn't acted like that since. And *other* women
had gone missing, ones whose remains could be skel-
etal by now.

Jo rolled her eyes at her own speculation. *She* was
getting spooked like any teenager to even imagine a
connection between the family cavern and the women
who'd disappeared.

Still, she had to do *something* to verify or discount
Jesse's story. If this incident had caused the alienation
between Rod and Lucy, there was a chance Jo might
be able to bring a close to it.

Except—that meant *she* had to venture into the forbidden part of the cavern on her own. Keeping her
intentions secret from Lucy unless she found something…and defying Rod. To whom Jo owed such a
debt.

She suddenly wished she could ask Alan to go with
her.

ALAN TOOK CALLS while he methodically drove one road
at a time across the quarter of the county he'd been al-
lotted. It was slow going, given that he also turned into
every driveway that disappeared into the trees, parked
and investigated derelict buildings, and stopped at turn-
outs to be sure a body hadn't been tossed from a vehicle and that there wasn't broken vegetation suggesting
anyone had driven deeper into the woods.

His phone rang just as he braked in front of a barn
that was one snowfall away from collapse. The double
doors hung crookedly, but there were enough cracks
between old, dried-up boards forming the siding that

he doubted he'd need to get a door open to survey the interior.

Staying behind the wheel, he answered the phone. "Burke."

"Alan, it's Drew. I've found another diver. He thinks he can give you the backup you need."

In other words, a recreational scuba diver had come forward. The guy probably had never descended past fifteen feet, and that in the clear waters of the Caribbean on a cruise ship excursion.

"Let me have his number," Alan said noncommittally. Diving alone was never a good idea, but he'd about resigned himself to doing so. Dropping far enough into the various deeper lakes, quarries and sinkholes in the area was unlikely to present much of a challenge—or risk—to him. Still, complacency wasn't a mistake he'd made since he'd been lucky enough to survive being a reckless kid. Anyone might be better than no one.

Even as he listened to Drew's answer, his gaze followed what looked like movement in the falling-down structure in front of him. An animal? Or had someone taken possession of this place for an unknown reason?

"Name's Edgar Madsen," Drew said. "I've met him before—he's a detective in Marion County across the border in Arkansas. Lots of lakes there." Drew hesitated. "We're striking out otherwise."

No surprise that a rural county in the middle of the country wasn't home to a host of passionate deep-sea divers.

Not taking his eyes from the barn, Alan said, "I'll

call and let you know." Then he opened his door and climbed out, dropping the phone in a pocket and reached for the handgun he carried in a holster on his belt. Staying behind the cover of the car door, he called, "Anyone here?"

Wood rattled followed by the crashing sound of someone—or something—running into the woods.

He dashed to the corner of the barn and peered around it. "I don't care if you're trespassing," he yelled. "You don't have to run away."

The sound of someone or something fleeing continued to recede. He grunted, holstered his weapon, and bent to peer between the heavy warped boards that made up the siding. Bands of light let him see the dirt floor, but the bulk of what might have been stalls or equipment left behind blocked his view of the whole space.

Instead of wrestling with the obvious entrance in front, he eased around the back. An ordinary-sized door stood open. He turned on the LED flashlight he'd carried in yet another pocket of his cargo pants, shone it in a wide arc, and stepped inside.

Two rusting pieces of farm equipment sat in the middle: a tractor and what he thought was an old harvester. Both were well past any chance of a second life. In a stall that stretched along one side of the barn, he found a setup that suggested someone was camping out here. An indentation in a heap of old straw; a bundle that he saw, after a nudge of his booted foot, held some sandwich makings, a few soup cans and a couple of battered paperbacks; and a wool blanket prickly with straw slung over the side of the stall.

He poked around the ground floor, found no sign of digging, and climbed partway up the ladder into the loft. Not trusting the brittle rungs, Alan swung himself the rest of the way. There wasn't much up there; using a rusting rake with a broken handle, he pushed the rotting remains of old straw or hay around to be sure no bodies or evidence of any other human presence were there.

Then he swung himself over the edge, landing hard and rolling. He took another look at the nest in the stall before going out to his pickup truck. Pity made him want to let sleeping dogs lie; it was probably a runaway or a homeless person camping out here, but he knew he couldn't not report what he'd discovered. Not with the possibility a serial killer had just abducted an innocent young woman.

After starting the engine, he kept an eye on the barn while he made two calls: one to the detective who turned out to have more diving experience than Alan had guessed, then to Drew himself.

ONCE SHE HAD her hands on the keys—and boy, did she feel like scum after searching Rod's bedroom—Jo's next dilemma was when she could search the gated passage without anyone's knowledge. She seriously considered asking Lucy to accompany her. Jo wasn't crazy about the idea of venturing beyond the tourist area of the cavern entirely alone, but she concluded that she couldn't trust Lucy to keep her mouth shut, and Brody...wasn't an option.

Sneaking out of the house in the middle of the night seemed problematic, plus gates were closed and locked at the mouth of the cavern at night, too. Put dinner on, then slip away while it was cooking? Problem was, Rod often lingered in his office in the gift shop longer than the rest of them, and several nights a week returned there after dinner, too.

So—during the day, Jo concluded, while Rod was leading a tour. She'd make an excuse to Brody and Lucy or anyone else who might wonder at her absence. She'd claim to have a headache, she decided, say she was going to take some prescription medication and lie down for an hour. Instead, she'd slip into the cavern on the heels of the tour. She should be able to get in and out during the hour before the tour returned. If memory served her, it wasn't that far to the spacious room with the shallow pool that Lucy had described.

She led the one o'clock tour herself. Rod was to take the next one.

She walked everyone into the gift shop and was still smiling, answering questions and thanking the people who'd accompanied her through the cavern when Rod approached.

"You okay?" he asked in a low voice.

Her anxiety had to be leaking out even though she hadn't yet had a chance to start acting. Oh, face it— she never had been very good at being sneaky or lying.

"Headache," she murmured back. "I'll be okay."

Eyes sharp on her face, he nodded.

Not ten minutes later, he had gathered the next tour group—a big one, probably twenty-five people—and led them into the maw of the cavern. She saw only Brody near enough to talk to and made her excuses to him, then slipped into the shadowed interior of the cavern close enough behind the tour to hear Rod's strong, confident voice and the group laughter he knew how to arouse.

The lights strung throughout were turned on, section by section, by the tour guide, then turned off as they moved on. At one point, halfway through the experience, those lights were all turned off just long enough to have the tourists squeaking and gasping when they found out what complete darkness looked like.

Jo slipped on her helmet with the headlamp as soon as she was certain no one would see her, and carried a flashlight besides. She just had to be sure Rod didn't catch so much as a glimpse of a beam of light where it didn't belong.

Heart pounding, she crept along the familiar path, smoothly paved but unfamiliar when she was relying only on the edges of the glow from the overhead electric lights well ahead. She had to keep reminding herself that she knew this route like the back of her hand. She ought to have been able to walk it blindfolded.

Nonetheless, she was glad when she reached the magnificent, twisting flow formation that served as an exquisite curtain to hide a metal gate sunk in concrete pilings. A second gate later on the tour was obvious, and that's where the tour guide would explain about the multiple passages that wound in a maze not yet entirely explored. Rod was especially good at talking about the secrets those as yet unseen passages might still guard: Spanish gold, illicit bullion stolen from a train robbery when the crime was common in the days of Jesse James, fossils, even the remnants of a Prohibition era still. He liked to hint that his own family, longtime owners of this land, had been up to some not yet revealed sins.

Jo had to turn on the headlamp to get the key in the lock without doing something dumb like dropping it. Once through the gate, she closed it as quietly as she could—but only after testing several times her ability to let herself *out*.

Once she turned her back on the gate, she faced the stunning darkness that always gave her a tiny frisson of fear even when she was the one to switch off the lights during the tour. Her eyes strained to see anything at all, and failed. She imagined eternal darkness if she went blind, and shuddered. No. She was comfortable in the cavern and caves in general from long experience, but she didn't love being underground the way Rod and Brody did.

A stray thought passed through her mind. Was Alan Burke a dedicated caver, too?

And why was she just *standing* there? Deadline, remember? Jo turned on her headlamp, inexpressibly relieved by the warm, broad beam that revealed the passage in front of her. It was easily ten feet high if somewhat narrower. Walking required dodging several stalactites hanging from the ceiling. She examined them as she passed, glad not to spot any damage.

Rubble covered the floor of this part of the cave, broken pieces of limestone, but nothing new that she could see. She bent to pass below an overhang that shone damply. An icy drop of water hit her neck, of course. She shivered as it trickled down her neck.

Beyond—she'd forgotten, but this was a primary reason Rod hadn't wanted to include any of this passage on the tour. To one side, nestled in a curve of the wall, was what looked for all the world like an undersea garden of coral. A helictite, defying the force of gravity, and perhaps the most fragile of cave formations. God, if Lucy or Brody had let any of their drunk friends damage *this*—

Jo stopped longer than she should have to shine her LED flashlight over the formation, as Rod had certainly done when he passed through here after learning about the parties. No damage, but she sympathized even more with his rage. He was right—protecting the fragile wonders beyond the tourist path was a responsibility she was glad he took seriously.

Deadline.

She moved as fast as she could now, with the limited light and the thick air and silence that wasn't quite silent. Whispers, murmurs, tiny drips, sighs. The cave talked, if you listened carefully enough. To someone unfamiliar with this environment, it would sound like ghosts.

It took her less than fifteen minutes to reach the Mirage Room, so named by Rod, although Jo hadn't thought about it in years until Lucy told her where she'd thrown her parties.

Somewhat like the famous Mirror Room at the Meramec Cavern, the water in a slow-moving stream that had spread to fill half the floor space appeared to have vast depths, reflecting the surfaces around it. In truth, it was only inches deep.

Jo stopped, sweeping her flashlight every direction, all but holding her breath. She could easily imagine a timid kid scared out of his wits once he'd been separated from his friends down here. If she heard the sepulchral barking of a dog, she'd probably jump out of her skin.

She rolled her eyes, pinpointed the dark outline of what looked like a skinny doorway and forced herself to continue.

As she'd remembered, the passage narrowed just enough to induce a hint of claustrophobia, but in something like fifteen feet it again widened and the ceiling rose, too, although this space was nowhere near as big as the Mirage Room. As if it was breathing, she could hear the water that ran through here, although *hear* might not be the right word, so soft was it. She could *feel* it, then.

A prize exhibition on the tour was a nest of cave pearls that appeared for all the world to be eggs laid in a nest. Jo had never heard of one big enough for even a sloshed kid to mistake for a skull. Yes, some rocks lay around, probably remnants of long-fallen limestone formations, but really this room was one that, at least in the beam of her headlight, seemed tinted orange. Not seemed: orange calcite wasn't uncommon in these limestone caverns.

Even as she kept an eye on the watch she wore when leading tours to keep her on schedule, she searched the periphery of the room. Nothing leaped out at her. Unfortunately, this was one of those spots where multiple passages opened up, and she remembered that one of those split a hundred yards or so farther along.

Tilting her head and concentrating, she decided she wasn't mistaken picking out a susurrating sound different than what she'd heard earlier. This seemed to rise and fall, as if someone was crying somewhere in the cavern.

Of course, that was just her brain trying to label a sound created by ancient forces within the earth, but... she had to know.

Gritting her teeth, she started for the first of the several passages.

Chapter Six

Alan splashed backward off the rock into the water of the sinkhole—a long-ago collapsed part of a cave system—as if he was entering from a boat. Persuading a car to drive off the rim would have been a job, but could have been done. And this water looked plenty deep enough to hide almost anything.

There wasn't much hope of finding the Kendall girl alive nearly a week after her disappearance, but Alan would do anything he could to help find the killer. This was the next step.

Exhaling into his regulator, he moved a short distance with easy movements of his ankles as he waited for his dive partner to enter behind him.

Alan had been reassured almost at first meeting with Detective Ed Madsen. Late-thirties, early forties, the guy was five foot ten or so and fit. The equipment he'd unloaded from his pickup looked both well used and well cared for. Decent quality, too; he'd invested some money in his hobby.

They'd shaken hands, evaluating each other as Drew Frazier looked on.

"You were really a navy SEAL?" Madsen asked. He had a noticeable accent, making Alan guess he was originally from a Deep South state.

"I was."

"Damn. I'm not often impressed, but I'll admit I am."

"No need," Alan said with a relaxed smile. "I don't think we'll be doing anything that will require my superpowers."

Madsen laughed. "Don't suppose. I keep up my skills by doing some diving in our local lakes. Used to do cave diving, too, but my partner moved away, and I haven't found anyone else I'd trust to join me."

They eyed each other. "I've done it in other parts of the world," Alan said, "but never locally." He'd missed being in the water, the escape from gravity and sense of solitude even with dive buddies. Yeah, he might enjoy some exploring if he could trust this man as backup.

Halfway through the day, he'd decided he had enough confidence in the detective to join him on an expedition through one of the flooded caverns in the Ozark area.

They'd already gone deep in another sinkhole to find a crack wide enough to have allowed passage that very possibly opened into a cave. The crack wasn't wide enough for a car to have scraped through, though, so they'd turned around and risen at a pace that allowed for a few safety stops back to the surface.

They'd actually located a rusting hulk of a pickup truck in a quarry first thing that morning. Alan had photographed a license plate that barely hung by one screw for Drew to identify the vehicle, but this truck had been down here too many years to be connected to any of the missing women.

In fact, Drew had been irritated, because that had been a favorite spot for teenagers to dive, and no one had ever reported the pickup.

"We'd better haul it out," he grumbled, "before some kid gets snagged exploring."

Alan wholeheartedly agreed. "Let me know if you need help once you get it arranged." Chains would have to be attached to the heap in places where the metal wouldn't just crumble off when any force was applied.

"Ditto," his diving partner agreed.

Now Madsen signaled to Alan and both men pulled the valve on their buoyancy control devices to begin a relaxed descent, shining their main dive lights in front of them. From long practice, he slowed the beating of his heart, leaving behind his stresses. This water was the cloudiest they'd seen yet. It was being fed from another source, Alan diagnosed, and pulled downward, possibly into another flooded cavern. Even so, the lights penetrated plenty far enough for them to move with confidence and reasonable speed.

Now and again, he paused to sweep the lights to each side, visually measuring the width of the sinkhole. It was narrowing, but only slightly, and they were already—he glanced at his dive computer—forty meters deep, and no bottom in sight.

This would be a hell of a place to make a vehicle disappear.

He tapped the computer on his wrist. Madsen looked

at his own and nodded his understanding. The only way they'd have time at this depth to evaluate anything was to plan for decompression stops as they surfaced, especially since this was their third dive of the day. No problem if they reached the bottom soon and saw nothing, but he knew of one flooded cave in the area that was considerably deeper than they'd yet gone.

And then his light picked out a shape that didn't belong, and he adjusted the angle of his flippers to take him straight at it.

It was a car, all right, a shiny red Ford Focus. Damn. Part of him hadn't wanted to find anything, but here it was. He snapped photos of the license plate, although he didn't have to. After getting involved in the hunt for the missing young woman, he'd memorized the plate number on her car.

While he did that, Madsen gestured to him, and he moved enough to see that the car rested atop a second one. He thought gray, but wasn't sure in the cloudy water, and saw signs of rusting. He and Madsen both photographed this license plate, too, before he shone his light at the abruptly narrowed walls of the hole to be sure there wasn't room for yet another vehicle to be down here. Then he took out his writing slate and scribbled a note for his partner to see.

Madsen gave a thumbs-up, and began a slow rise to look inside the windows of the Ford Focus while Alan did the same with this Pontiac. He was taking the greater risk; if Madsen bumped the Focus he could dislodge it.

After sweeps with the light, Alan saw nothing in the car. Not even a lump that might have been a woman's handbag. He was tempted to open the trunk, but decided not to. When he inhaled enough to rise, he saw that Madsen, too, had taken out a slate and written, *Trunk?*

Alan shook his head. The detective didn't argue. Both knew these cars would have to be raised from the water depths. Any remaining questions could be answered then. Alan didn't expect to find any bodies in the car trunks. Odds were that someone trying to ditch a dead woman along with a vehicle would have seat belted her in behind the wheel to confuse the issue of whether she might have chosen this death.

The ascent was slow, his patience with the decompression stops next to nonexistent. His mind worked the entire way, as he felt sure Ed Madsen's did as well. They were both cops, official today or not, and knew what this discovery meant.

He didn't like knowing how scared Jo Summerlin would be to hear what they'd found. She had to be feeling protective where her brother was concerned—but Alan found himself wondering how viable a suspect Brody was. If, as Alan suspected, this second car had belonged to the first woman to disappear, Brody would have been only sixteen years old. Okay, almost seventeen, but that was really young to commit this kind of crime. Foolishly, he wanted to share what they'd found today with Jo—but he had no business undercutting the investigation.

ONCE HE HEARD the news and studied the photos on both men's underwater cameras, Drew had made several calls, starting with the sheriff and ending with the owner-operator of a local tow company that had hauled smashed cars up from deep chasms. Underwater was new to the guy, but once reassured that volunteer divers would hook up the chains, he agreed to give it a try.

Given that he and Madsen shouldn't dive again until morning, Alan wished Drew had held off on making that call. He tended not to trust anyone to keep quiet with juicy news, but he didn't say anything. The very fact that he was again having to remind himself this wasn't his investigation made him conscious of a faint itch that told him he wished it was. Especially since he hadn't been impressed by anything he'd heard about the sheriff's department detective.

He and Madsen waited to one side, both listening to Drew's side of the phone calls. There'd been a time Alan wouldn't have hesitated to go back down again, no problem, but he hadn't done any diving in the past year, and the detective looked spent to Alan's eye.

"We haven't had any women disappear from my county," Madsen said out of the blue. "I was counting my blessings when Frazier first called, but now…"

Alan made a sound of agreement. He'd feel a lot better about this had any of the crimes been conducted in Madsen's backyard. At least he respected his new diving partner. Unfortunately, now that abduction had been confirmed, Detective Jantz would take over lead on the investigation from Drew.

Drew got off the phone and walked over to them. "We're set for nine in the morning."

Both nodded.

Looking grim, Drew added, "I got a hit on the second license plate number. Not a surprise. The car disappeared along with Christy Dodswell four years ago. She's the one from Newton County, the missing woman we tentatively connected with the others."

Not tentative anymore. Finding the two cars dumped in the same place tied those two missing women together despite the lengthy gap between their abductions. And with those two linked—

Ed Madsen said what all three of them were thinking. "We have a serial killer."

"Looks like it." Drew rubbed a hand over his face. "Sheriff wants us to keep it quiet as long as possible so we don't start a panic, but I don't think that's possible."

Madsen gave a sharp laugh. "Who does he think he's kidding? Even if the crew from the tow truck company keeps their mouths shut, you'll be hauling the two vehicles to—what?—department impound? If I remember right, it's in town surrounded by chain link fencing. Anyone going by will see in. You're going to have to notify the two families. The sheriff plans to try to stifle *them*?"

Alan hoped the sheriff's motivation had nothing to do with his reelection campaign. When nobody commented, Drew shook hands with both Madsen and Alan. "Can't thank you two enough."

"Any way I can contribute," Madsen said, before heading to his pickup.

Alan echoed him. "I think I'll stop for a bite in town. If you want to join me—?"

Drew grimaced. "I'll need to go see the Kendall girl's parents. Don't care what the sheriff thinks. They deserve to know what we've found."

"You wouldn't want them to hear from someone else," Alan agreed. "I'd suggest you try to keep them away in the morning, though. It'll be a long, hard job, and if her body turns out to be in the trunk…"

Drew swore under his breath. "Seeing her like that might kill them."

Privately, Alan couldn't help thinking that might almost be easier on the people who loved the girl than being left wondering what she was enduring—or never knowing what had happened to her. Drew was bound to have the same thoughts, though.

They parted ways, Alan not envying his childhood friend the duty that lay in front of him. He'd given terrified people the same kind of news in the years he'd served on the police force. Had to be the worst part of the job.

THE FIRST Jo heard was a voice coming from around the end cap at the grocery store.

"I hear they're diving, looking for her body."

Jo stopped her cart in front of spices, even though she didn't need any.

"It would float right up, wouldn't it?" said another woman. "And why would anyone expect her to have been dumped in a lake?"

It would be Alan Burke doing the diving, wouldn't

it? Everyone knew he'd been a SEAL. The sheriff wouldn't hesitate to take advantage of Alan's expertise, would he? She had no reason to know much about the sheriff.

The two women's voices had dropped, and Jo was just about to resume her shopping when a third person evidently joined them.

"Well, *I* heard they found something!" Another woman, and this one sounded triumphant about being in the know. "Not *they*. It was that Burke man, the one whose father sold methamphetamine." Spite infused her voice. "Of all people for our police to trust. If she's dead in the water, who's to say *he* didn't put her there in the first place?"

There might have been a polite rebuke, but if so the hateful woman overrode it. "Anyway, that deputy Frazier called Jed Chapman about him using his equipment to pull something out of the water."

"Why would they need a tow truck if they found a body?" one of the women asked with refreshing common sense.

"Well, her car is missing, too, isn't it?"

Chilled, Jo wondered if there was anything to this new report. If it was true, it was spreading awfully fast. Although, it would surely be better to have any answer as to what had become of Amy than to have none, wouldn't it?

What Jo hated was the tone of what she'd heard. Did that nasty woman think being able to spread news before anyone else could was more important than a local girl's well-being? Or that of her family? Indignant, Jo turned her cart around, grabbed a bottle of olive oil off the shelf, and kept going. She didn't want to see those women's faces. She'd be too tempted to say something scathing and make enemies for the Summerlin family. Rod wouldn't appreciate that.

She rushed through the store despite the risk of forgetting something, and loaded the trunk of her car without so much as turning her head to see who else came out on her heels. With luck, she wouldn't recognize those women, anyway. One of the first two voices had sounded familiar—a friend's mother, maybe, or someone who'd worked at the school?—but the most distinctive didn't ring any bells for her. God—think how horrible it would be if Amy's mother had been shopping and *this* was how she received the news! Jo hoped someone was doing all of the basic chores for the Kendall family, and that they weren't the kind to be determined to follow the routine of their days no matter what.

Jo turned out of the parking lot, intending to make a stop at the hardware store before going home, but the sight of a giant pickup truck parked at the curb in front of Ralph's Café changed her mind. Big black pickups weren't uncommon in these parts, but she'd seen Alan Burke drive away from the search in one just like this. Plus it had—yes!—Virginia license plates. She parallel parked as soon as she saw a spot, grabbed her purse and walked back to the café. In only half a block, she passed two Missing posters, one stapled to a pole, the other in a store window. Would putting Amy's face out there like this help? Jo shivered.

She saw Alan the minute she entered the café. He was the only person sitting alone, having claimed a booth in the back corner. He saw her as quickly.

Waving at the waitress, Jo hurried to Alan's booth. "May I join you?" she asked.

The pause might have been her imagination, but the resignation on his face when he said, "Of course," wasn't.

Tough.

"Was it you diving today?"

His expression was well locked down now. "It was."

"I heard at the grocery store—"

Crud, there was Wendy Smith, who'd been a waitress here since Jo was a little girl. She approached the table with a menu for Jo.

"Cup of coffee?" she asked.

"Make it iced tea."

"Okey doke." Wendy nodded at Alan. "Your food will be out any minute, honey."

Alan didn't react to the "honey," saying only "thanks." But he raised his eyebrows at Jo as soon as the waitress was out of earshot. "The grocery store?"

"Three women talking. One said she'd heard that you'd found two cars in, I don't know, a sinkhole or lake."

He scowled. "Damn. Did you see who it was?"

Jo shook her head. "They were out of sight. The woman sounded so hateful, I didn't want to know who she is."

"Hateful? About the missing women?"

Oh, heavens. She shouldn't have said that. But now

that she had… She took a deep breath. "She implied you might be responsible for dumping the cars as well as finding them. Because of your father."

He wiped away all expression again, which hurt to see. Jo would wish she hadn't said that, except he'd be bound to hear someone else expressing the same opinions.

"Your father wasn't violent, was he?"

"Nosy, are you?"

She made a face. "I know it's none of my business."

"It isn't," he said. "Yes, he was. Beat the tar out of my mother and me regularly. Cops came out a few times. Never found his meth lab, but they locked him up twice that I remember for fights at the bar, or maybe walloping a customer who didn't pay him. Not sure. Nothing like what's happening now, but if he were still alive, the cops might be looking at him."

She swallowed. "Oh."

Before she could think of anything sympathetic or even halfway intelligent to say, Wendy showed up with his burger and fries as well as Jo's iced tea, refilled his coffee and only nodded when Jo declined to order food.

Alan started eating as if the topic of conversation hadn't been at all disturbing.

Jo dumped a packet of sugar into the iced tea, stirred it and finally said, "I'm sorry."

His big shoulders moved. "Long time ago."

She met his eyes. "Some things never feel as if they happened long enough ago."

A tip of his head conceded her point. He grabbed a fry and dipped it in catsup.

Apparently he wasn't going to volunteer any news. Since word—true or not—was already spreading, Jo wasn't about to go home without finding out what had been found.

"*Did* you find two cars?"

Alan sighed. "We did. I'm sorry, Amy Kendall's was one of them. The other belonged to another of the missing women."

"Oh, God. That means they're both dead, doesn't it?"

"Christy Dodswell, almost certainly yes." He grimaced. "I shouldn't have told you that name. It'll get around soon enough, but I'm asking you not to repeat that to anyone."

Stunned even though this had always been the likely outcome, Jo nodded. It would probably take a while to notify Christy's family, and that was assuming they hadn't moved away.

"Amy…" Alan continued in that gritty voice. "Who knows? We didn't find bodies. She could still be alive."

It might be trite, but wasn't it also true that where there's life, there's hope? At this moment, though, Jo wasn't so sure, not when she could imagine the horrific things Amy might be suffering.

"I don't suppose they can get fingerprints or anything like that off cars that have been immersed in water for any length of time," she heard herself say.

"Unlikely. Unless the guy dropped something that survived…" Alan shook his head. "All finding the cars really tells us is that we have one perpetrator, and when something works, he repeats it."

"But…what about the other missing women's cars?"

She couldn't remember details about the other abductions.

"Not all of the women were driving when they disappeared. One vehicle was locked up and left beside the road not far from her house."

Jo leaned forward. "Wouldn't that have been the smart thing to do? I mean, unless he was on foot, it must have taken a long time to make a victim's vehicle disappear."

"Yes, except if someone happened to come along right after he snatched a girl and the police acted fast enough, that would up his risk."

"I...suppose so," Jo said slowly.

"Also, having the car gone clouded the issue. Had people thinking she might have just taken off."

Also true.

Alan chewed and swallowed a bite of his burger before saying, "So, you stopped by just to interrogate me?"

Heat rose to her cheeks. "I...was curious."

"I noticed that about you already."

"What?"

His amusement became apparent. "You weren't about to let me go in that cave by myself. What I saw, you wanted to see, too." Except, suddenly, the smile in his eyes was gone. "Unless you've been thinking like the woman at the grocery store all along. Why wouldn't anyone belonging to the Burke family be a logical suspect? What if I'd stashed the body in that cave?"

Chapter Seven

The shock on Jo Summerlin's face felt like a fist in the gut to Alan. Damn it, why had he said anything like that? He knew better. Even after such a short time, he knew *her* better.

"Jo."

"You think I'm like that?" She scooted fast across the vinyl bench seat to get away from him. "What have I ever said—?"

"Stop." He half rose. "Please. I'm sorry. I…lashed out for no reason." No reason? Or had he been hurt by even a faint possibility she agreed with the common local opinion?

She's not for me, remember?

Instead of getting to her feet, she hesitated, her eyes searching his.

"I came in here looking for you because I was mad about what that woman said." Her voice trembled just a little. "I would never believe something like that. I've always hated the idea that we're predestined to be like our parents. *I* would never—"

She broke off so suddenly he didn't learn what she

would never do. Whatever it was, it involved hurting another person, and she was too compassionate to do that if she could help it.

After the things he'd done, whether in theory he'd been on the side of good in the battle with evil or not, he didn't belong at the same table with her. And yet, she drew him powerfully, and he hated knowing that, at the very least, what he'd said had stung.

"I…let myself get sensitive," he made himself admit. "I'm getting a lot of that attitude from townspeople, even ones who knew me as a kid."

Her forehead crinkled. "Were you a delinquent as a child?"

He shook his head. "A little wild, maybe. I didn't like to go home any more than I could help, so I did some trespassing. Got caught sleeping in someone's car or barn a few times. I wasn't the best student back then."

To his astonishment, she reached across the table and laid her hand over his. "Were you glad to go live with your grandparents?"

"Yeah." He had to clear some hoarseness from his throat. "I felt guilty about leaving my mother, but… yeah."

"She was an adult."

"I know." He did. Even then, he'd realized he couldn't do anything for her. She wasn't just terrorized by his dad, she was using by then, probably to dull the reality of her life. Alan would be forever grateful that she'd had the courage to defy his father by sending him away.

To his regret, Jo took her hand back. He wasn't much

accustomed to someone expressing sympathy with a physical gesture, especially when that someone was a beautiful woman.

God, he thought; what if the killer had happened on her during one of her visits home these past few years? Alan would never have met her. Not that he could see a relationship with her going anywhere. Except…she was tougher than he'd first imagined, and for whatever reason, she fired up his protective instincts.

Maybe, it occurred to him, because they had at least one quality in common. He had no doubt she'd be fierce in defense of the people she believed in. Or in her case, he should probably say loved. Pure nosiness didn't explain her determination to stay on top of the investigation; no, she was worrying about her brother's connection to the latest victim.

She let out a sigh and scooted back toward the middle of her side of the booth. "You should eat. I'm sorry if I ruined your meal. If you want me to leave…"

Alan shook his head and smiled crookedly. "Having a pretty woman keeping me company never spoils a meal for me."

She wrinkled her nose at him. "Do you have any idea what the police will do next?"

He guessed she was trying to get them back on an even keel. "For starters, pull the cars out of the sinkhole. Go over them with a fine-tooth comb."

"Will you be helping them with that?"

"I and a deputy from Arkansas will dive to hook the chains in place so the tow truck can haul them up.

Otherwise…" He hesitated. "I guess I'm out of it, unless any more searches are organized."

Jo nodded her understanding.

"They'll start an investigation," he continued. "Find out if Amy and Christy had anything in common. Who might have known both?" Although there was no saying that the killer had known any of the victims in advance. They might simply have caught his eye when they were vulnerable.

"Christy wasn't local, was she?" Jo asked.

"Another county, but not that far away." He had a vague recollection. "I think she was a cheerleader."

Jo looked dismayed. "Amy was, too."

"There you go."

Come to think of it, he hadn't heard where Christy had been when abducted. Near home? Or was there some chance she'd been around Mayville? Did anybody know, given that her car hadn't been found at the time?

"But…were Amy and Christy close enough in age to have known each other?"

He should quit thinking out loud, Alan realized. He was forced to yet again confront the fact that this investigation wasn't his, despite his certainty he could handle it better than the unimaginative, by-the-books and near-retirement detective for the sheriff's department. The one who'd opposed searching for Amy at all. It was to the sheriff's credit that he'd let Drew run with it.

After the cops Alan had worked with and trusted had failed so badly in his estimation with such tragic consequences, he'd been sure he was done with law enforcement. Could be he'd been wrong. Assuming his boss in his previous department gave a decent recommendation that would give him a shot at a job with a different department, that was.

"There might have been a connection that didn't have anything to do with age," he felt compelled to say. Jo had babysat Amy, for example, knowing the girl well enough to grieve now, despite the span of years between them. "Besides, whether they knew each other or not isn't the point."

"It's who else they both knew," she finished.

"Yes. Maybe. Although these could have been crimes of opportunity."

They looked at each other again in the unguarded way that made him feel naked. Alan didn't know how she did that, or whether he was imagining it. But, damn it, she got to him as no one had in a long time.

"I'm scared," she said quietly. "I mean, this is a small town. I know most people. Or at least, I did. You—"

He arched an eyebrow. "Feel safe?" There was irony, when she felt anything *but* safe to him.

"No-o." Color brushed her cheeks.

Along with the blushing was a shyness that surprised him, even as it stirred his body uncomfortably. So "safe" didn't describe how she felt when she was with him. Well, he didn't feel all that safe with her, either, except in a literal sense. Certainly, in the cave Jo had exuded a confidence and competence that had relaxed him.

"Jo—" He was going to do something foolish. He knew he was. Asking her out wouldn't be good for either of them, but damn, he wanted to get to know this woman.

"I should be going." She slid out of the booth quicker than he could draw a breath. Her eyes wouldn't quite meet his. "I have groceries in the car. I shouldn't have dawdled this long. Anyway, I'm the cook tonight, and it's getting late."

Alan had a feeling she was the cook every night while she was home, but maybe he was wrong.

"Okay," he said, wanting to be glad she was fleeing before he could make a stupid suggestion. "Remember what you promised."

"Promised?" Comprehension had her casting a quick look around her. Even so, she lowered her voice. "You mean Christy. I keep promises."

"I...have no doubt you do," he said, something in his voice he hardly understood. Intimacy? Trust deeper than it should have been? If that was it, he had to shut it down. Now. "I may see you around," he said brusquely.

A flicker in her eyes was Jo's only reaction. Then she dropped a five-dollar bill on the table and walked away.

None of the rest of the family was home when Jo got there. She carried the groceries in, realized Rod would be annoyed that she'd forgotten to stop at the hardware store and shrugged it off. Too bad. He could grab what he needed the next time he was out. After putting the food away, she started dinner—spaghetti, a perennial favorite.

All three arrived together. Rod grinned at her as he walked into the kitchen. "Smells great."

Lucy wrinkled her nose. "Do we *have* to have broccoli?"

Brody bumped her with his shoulder. "Can it, kid, unless you want to take over cooking duties. And please, God, let that not happen."

"You're a jerk," his sister told him.

Wait until they were all sitting down? Jo asked herself, and decided, *No.* She did dump the spaghetti noodles into the boiling water, then turned to face them.

"I heard something in town."

Her tone killed the good humor on all three faces.

"They found Amy's car today. It was at the bottom of a sinkhole. Or maybe a lake, I'm not sure."

"Damn," her stepfather said, sounding shocked. "I really wanted to think—"

Jo nodded. "We all did."

Lucy was still gaping. Brody's hands closed into tight fists.

"Was…*she* in the car?"

Lucy whimpered.

"Not the way I heard it," Jo said. She turned down the heat under the spaghetti and the broccoli both.

"How did you hear?" Rod asked.

"Some women talking at the grocery store." Tell them about her conversation with Alan? No. Rod would disapprove of her being friendly to this neighbor who was thwarting his ambitions.

"So…someone went diving?" That was Brody again.

"Alan Burke. He was a SEAL, you know. The police were probably grateful to have someone with his diving experience available. I think maybe there was someone else, too." Wasn't that what Alan had implied, mentioning some guy from Arkansas?

Her stepfather snorted. "Burke. Why's *he* so eager to help?"

"He spent years in the military," she said as mildly as she could, considering her reaction to his contempt. "And I understand that he's been a cop since he got out of the navy."

Another sound, this one deeper in his throat, and Rod said, "Let's wash up."

Tears trembled on Lucy's lashes. "But...how can we just *eat*? Amy must be dead!"

Her brother turned on her. "Don't say that! Maybe—" His throat worked. "Maybe..."

In the absence of any help from the rest of the family, Jo stepped forward and hugged him, this solidly built young man she wasn't always sure she knew very well but who was her brother. His arms came around her and he hugged her back, hard. When he stepped away, his expression was tormented and his eyes wet, too.

"Amy...she's—she was—so sweet."

"I know," Jo whispered.

Predictably, Lucy broke out sobbing, whirled and ran for the stairs. A moment later, they all heard her door slam. Rod grumbled under his breath before saying, "She'll get hungry later."

"This is an easy dinner to reheat," Jo agreed, ignoring the lump in her own throat.

Brody stomped to the cupboard and got out dishes to set the table. Typical guy, she thought; he didn't let his emotions get in the way of meals.

She wished she didn't still feel that tiny bit of…oh, not suspicion, call it *apprehension*, when she thought about Brody and Amy, even though Brody couldn't possibly have had anything to do with Christy Dodswell's abduction. He'd been only sixteen, or was it seventeen? Anyway, how could he have met her? He hadn't even had his own car that long ago, had he?

No, she should be ashamed that she'd ever, for one minute, wondered about her own brother.

BRODY LEFT THE HOUSE right after dinner, as he so often did. Meeting up with friends, Jo assumed. Rod never commented on it, at least not in her hearing. The one evening she'd announced that everyone could heat up their own choice of leftovers, his irritation was obvious, but he'd managed to use the microwave. Tonight, Rusty excitedly accompanied Brody to his old pickup truck. Jo wished her brother would buy a new muffler for it.

Rod thanked her for cooking, kissed her on the cheek and said, "I still have work to do," and left the house, too. He hadn't gotten past the front porch when she heard yet another excited woof from the dog followed by Rod swearing. The front door opened and closed again, this time emphatically, and Rusty dashed for the kitchen, claws clicking on the worn hardwood floor. Jo hustled to clear the table, not sure she trusted the dog not to plant his paws on one of the chairs and slurp up any leftovers.

Sometimes Rod drove away, too, seeing the lady friend, she assumed, but most often, as he did tonight, he walked back to his office in the gift shop building. Apparently he hadn't wanted company. Rod didn't seem all that fond of the dog. He wasn't much of an animal person; he and her mother both shook their heads at her pleas to have a pet when she was young. Lucy and Brody were lucky he'd agreed to let them keep the young dog when he showed up as a stray.

She enjoyed Rusty's companionship as she cleaned the kitchen—didn't it figure this had been Lucy's night to handle the job—and went so far as to set a plate down with some leftovers before she put a plate for Lucy and the remaining leftovers into the refrigerator. She should have grabbed Brody and asked for help with clean up before he got out the door. Once she started the dishwasher, Jo sighed and headed for the stairs. What she wanted was to take a hot bath and then shut herself into her own room, but Lucy needed her whether she knew it or not.

She knocked on her sister's door.

"Jo?"

"It's me."

The tear-choked voice said, "You can come in."

Rusty had followed Jo, of course, and he pushed in as well and rushed to his girl, who went to her knees on the rug and threw her arms around the dog. Jo sat on the edge of the bed next to them.

"I wanted to be sure you're okay."

Lucy gave her a distraught look. "How can I be?"

"I know you're upset, but you weren't that close to Amy."

"No, but—" Her breath hitched.

"She was part of what should have been a safe world." Jo remembered feeling the same after her mother abandoned her.

Lucy's head bobbed.

When Jo stroked her hair, the teenager kept one arm around the dog but also leaned against Jo's leg. "It's just so awful."

"I know."

"And…and I know that skull didn't have anything to do with Amy, because she was still alive when Jesse found it, but…it's so *creepy*."

Yes, it was. Jo would give a lot to know what had excited Rusty so much the night Amy was abducted. Imagining some kind of connection was probably ridiculous, but the timing niggled at her.

Fortunately, she could at least partially reassure Lucy. Jo hadn't had a chance to talk to her sister yesterday evening. That was part of the reason she'd been determined tonight.

"I got the key and went in the cave," she said.

"What?" Lucy sat up straight and turned to allow herself to see Jo's face.

"I told you I'd try. Yesterday, when I said I had a headache, I slipped in once the tour passed that gate. I went to where Jesse said he saw the skull, and then farther yet. Several passages separate there, you know. I went a little ways into all of them." Hurriedly, but she didn't say that. "I didn't find anything, any more than your dad did. And that deputy he said he took with him," she added. "Was that Drew Frazier?"

"Uh-uh. It was Deputy Hudson. I didn't like him. And I don't think he really wanted to go into the cavern at all, but he wouldn't admit *he* was scared."

Jo hadn't seen enough of the stocky cop to say she didn't like him, but she hadn't been impressed. And he did look like the kind who wouldn't want anyone to suspect he had any weaknesses whatsoever.

"That wouldn't be a shock. A lot of men are like that."

"I guess." Lucy was quiet for a minute. "You're *sure*?"

"I'm sure there was nothing like a skull or any kind of bones when I went looking," she said. "Honestly, not even a rock that looked remotely *like* a skull. I guess Rusty could have carried something off, but he couldn't exactly bury it in a hole back there."

"No." The teenager's face scrunched in thought, even as she studied her big sister. "You think Jesse imagined it, don't you?"

Jo hesitated, but finally said, "I do. *He* could have been spooked by the cave, you know. If he was drunk…"

"Except he wasn't that drunk," Lucy said softly. "And he was totally freaked out. I wish… I should have gone to see for myself, but… I guess I was scared."

"I don't blame you." Jo made a face. "Don't tell anybody, especially Brody, but I didn't enjoy poking around. I don't mind leading the tours, but I've never wanted to go exploring."

"Me, either. Brody's jealous that he's never had the

chance to learn to dive, because he wants to be able to go into caves with passages that are underwater. Can you *imagine*?"

Sump diving. In Jo's opinion, exploring that kind of cave was particularly unappealing, if only because it involved dry stretches where you'd have to carry a hundred plus pounds of air tanks and all the other gear required for the underwater parts, and then you had to figure out how to squeeze the tanks through narrow spots. What if you got through, but the tanks wouldn't fit? The idea made her shudder.

She'd bet Alan Burke wouldn't think twice about joining something like the search for the kids and their coach trapped in the flooded cave in Thailand a few years ago.

She needed to quit imagining him as a hero. Who knew, he might have been fired from his last job as a cop. Nobody had said. There had to be a reason he didn't seem to be working.

Bringing herself back to the moment, she said, "I'm sorry to have brought the news about Amy. It's really hard to imagine something like that happening here. We think we know everyone."

Lucy bobbed her head. "It makes me kind of afraid to go anywhere by myself. You know?"

"You should be extra careful." Jo didn't want to terrify a girl who was at an age where she needed to be asserting her independence, but this was a good time for her to stick close to home.

"Why? I don't really fit. The girls that disappeared have all been lots older."

Early twenties didn't seem to be "lots older" than a sixteen-year-old to Jo, but all she said was, "Their ages might be chance. Because the missing women were old enough to do things like drive home alone from college for a school break."

Lucy hugged herself, her eyes huge. She said suddenly, "I'm glad you're here."

Jo gave a shaky smile. "Me, too."

With something that might have been a sob, Lucy pushed herself up to her knees and threw herself at Jo, who closed her arms around this sister whose certainties had been shattered.

She didn't think Lucy cried, but they stayed like that for a couple of minutes.

Finally, she murmured, "What do you say we go downstairs and I'll warm up some spaghetti for you?"

Lucy took a deep breath and slowly separated herself. "Is Dad still here? Or Brody?"

"Neither."

"Oh. Okay. Thanks."

As Jo heated leftovers a few minutes later, she tried to decide whether she dared raise the subject of the tension between Lucy and her father. Her conclusion: no. She'd had a breakthrough with her sister already. Why spoil the one step forward with two back?

Anyway, she understood. She hadn't had an easy relationship with Rod, either. Most of the time, he was brusque and uninterested in talking out any issues. Like a lot of men, he was probably just more comfortable with boys versus girls.

Assailed by renewed guilt, Jo regretted having failed

to notice any change in Lucy's emotional state until Rod called asking for help. Well, from here on out, she'd be paying much closer attention, she vowed. Her sister still needed her more than Jo had realized.

Chapter Eight

Alan wasn't worried for himself. He'd made an automatic evaluation of the possibility that a piece of machinery as heavy as a car not resting on a solid foundation would shift at a mere bump, or even because the water around it was disturbed. He'd done a lot more dangerous work underwater than hooking the axle of a car so it could be raised to the surface. His main concern was that Madsen's experience with diving was all recreational. He lacked the experience to judge the risks, and the ability to avoid so much as brushing the car unnecessarily. Alan wished he'd told Ed to leave this part up to him, to stick to providing backup. It was too late now, though.

Amy Kendall's Ford Focus had settled with the back bumper sitting atop the trunk of the vehicle below it, much of the undercarriage seemingly lying on the roof of the other car, so that the nose tipped upward. The position encouraged them to think they had easy access to the front axle. Alan never trusted a promise of easy.

He had his eye on Ed, who was already under there, a hook in his hand, dragging the heavy duty chain behind him. Ed was to secure one side of the axle, Alan the other. Damn, he'd feel better if the car sat solidly on a rocky bed, but as long as they were careful—

The car lurched, brushing his shoulder. Alarm ignited his instincts. He finned backward. Ed had either come in contact with a fender, or the heavy chain pulling over the front bumper had upset the delicate balance. Had he felt the movement?

Shoving back at an out-of-body instant, Alan dropped his hook and went after his partner. He grabbed Madsen's ankle and yanked backward. Metal was probably squealing, but sound was muffled down here. He felt as if he was moving in slow motion. What if there wasn't enough time to get Ed out?

But at his touch, the other man reacted instantly by curling away from the car and, with a couple of hard flicks of his fins, placing himself at a safe distance. Heart beating a hell of a lot harder than it should be, Alan joined him in watching the small red car slide in slow motion until it lay almost on its side, but still resting against the other car. Given a ten- or twenty-second difference in reaction time, Ed could have been crushed by metal on each side.

Damn, Alan thought. He was breathing harder than was safe at this depth. He knew better. The movement had stirred up increased debris in the water, too, impairing his ability to tell whether Ed was shaken up. Grimly, Alan set about slowing his own breathing, taking control of the speed of his pulse. Madsen did have enough experience to be doing the same thing himself.

Finally, Alan drifted closer to the car again, aware that the detective was with him.

He flattened a hand on the roof and shoved. The bottom was far from flat, but he felt no new movement. Ed tried the same by pushing on the bumper. He looked toward Alan, who gestured toward the dangling hooks.

He took hold of his again, this time maneuvering into position to use the self-locking hook to secure the chain around the low side of the axle. Once he'd backed out, Ed swam close and got the second hook in place.

This time, they eased over to the guide rope they were using to communicate with the people above. Knowing how likely screwups were, Alan had insisted on a way to send signals. Good thing, because the initial chains dropped had come up short despite Alan having shared the exact depth yesterday.

He and Ed had been forced to hover down here waiting, trusting that Drew Frazier, at least, was monitoring the rope and remembered that an emphatic two yanks translated to *doesn't reach the car*.

Now he gave one hard pull. *We're coming up.*

Their ascent would be slower than the car's, given the decompression stops they had to make, but he wasn't taking the chance of the damn thing being raised ahead of them. What if it broke free from the chains? The sinkhole was too narrow for them to be sure they could get out of the way. This wasn't the kind of thing Alan left to chance.

A good long while later, he hauled himself out of the water and signaled the go-ahead to Drew Frazier and the tow truck operator. Creaking, cranking noises began as the winch turned, and the chains grew taut. He'd been impressed earlier to see how hefty this tow truck was. It included a good-sized boom and a flatbed that was hydraulically operated so that a car could be pulled right onto it and lifted for transport. The whole setup wasn't all that different from ones used by the military, although those tended to be armored, too.

Ed Madsen crawled right up beside Alan. He wrestled free of his tanks, flopped onto his back and tore his mask off his head. "Son of a bitch. That was fun, and we get to do it again tomorrow."

Alan shared the sentiment. Even assuming all went well now, bringing the first car up had eaten up too much time. He had no intention of taking a relatively inexperienced diver back down again today.

Wrestling the tanks with all the attached gear off his back, Alan watched Jed Chapman, a bulky, balding guy, operate the winch while his assistant leaned over the sinkhole waiting for the car to come into sight. Drew and the sheriff's department detective hovered right beside him.

The lip of the sinkhole was rocky. The boom was adjustable, allowing them to winch the car almost straight up so it hung like a mighty big fish on a line before it was slowly maneuvered over the flatbed of the truck. Metal screamed. Water ran off the car and out of it, spilling in every direction. Jed and the assistant stayed intensely focused, adjusting it in the air, until it landed with a thud and some final rocking on the flatbed, tire side down.

They produced tie-down straps, but waited for Drew

to open the unlocked driver's side door of the little red car and find the lever to release the trunk latch. They'd all waited for this moment. Detective Jantz was the first to position himself at the back to get a good look inside the trunk.

Figured.

Jantz looked irritated when Ed and Alan stepped forward as the trunk lid rose, but even he must have decided he couldn't say much after the work they'd put in to find and bring the missing girl's car to the surface.

There was a kind of belching noise before the trunk lid lifted high enough to let them see in. The space was full of water. Something blue floated on the surface, obscuring their view. Drew fished it out with one gloved hand. A raincoat. Below that, there wasn't anything but the bump of a spare tire.

No dead girl. No obvious weapons. No clue.

Alan might have been disappointed at the whole lot of nothing, except he hadn't expected anything else, and he assumed Drew and even Jantz weren't any more surprised.

Amy Kendall, alive or dead, was somewhere else.

He turned to Drew. "This took too long. We can't go back down until morning."

His friend looked disappointed but nodded his understanding, while Jantz said, "What the hell? We've got the whole day ahead of us! Maybe we can get some other divers."

Alan just looked at him. "Good luck with that. If I don't hear from you to the contrary, I'll see you all at the same time tomorrow morning."

Without waiting for a response, he walked over to pick up his tanks, light, flippers and weights. Out of the corner of his eye, he saw Ed was doing the same. Within minutes, both peeled off their black neoprene wetsuits, scrubbed wet hair with towels they'd brought, and pulled on jeans and sweatshirts. Neither spared so much as a glance toward Detective Jantz, who shared some intense words with Drew before stomping over to his official vehicle, getting in and taking off with a spurt of dirt and gravel.

Probably wanted to be the first to share what little they'd gleaned with the sheriff.

"I had a close call down there," Ed remarked as he finished tossing his gear into the back of his SUV and slammed the hatch. "Thanks for the quick warning."

"You're welcome."

The Arkansas detective opened the door and got in. "Let's hope tomorrow goes more smoothly."

"Amen. But hey, today could have been worse."

Ed grinned crookedly. Yeah, he could have been crushed. "You suppose Jantz will bother getting up early tomorrow morning?"

Alan glanced toward Drew, who was now talking to the tow truck operator. "I'm betting not."

"You and me both." Ed shut his door, fired up the engine and lifted a hand to Alan, who guessed he ought to exchange a few words with Drew before he took off, too.

He didn't like that he wished he had an excuse to see Jo today. What would she have said yesterday if he'd suggested meeting for lunch again instead of shutting her down the way he had?

JO DIDN'T SEE much of her sister as the day went on. She
assumed that was by chance; they both took turns as
tour guide, barista, gift store clerk and just wandering,
indoors and out, to answer questions. Business had accelerated this week, with most school districts out. Rod
was in a good mood all day, so he must be happy with
the take from tickets and sales.

Jo was somewhat distracted, too, thinking about
the operation to raise the two cars from the bottom
of the sinkhole. Was the job done? Had they found
anything in either car? She didn't want to think about
what would happen to a body immersed in water for
close to a week, never mind one down there for several years. If the body was trapped in the trunk, at least
there wouldn't be damage from fish or who knows
what nibbling—

That was as far as she let herself get. She didn't *want*
to know how a dead person decomposed in water or
anywhere else.

She did want to know whether either victim had been
found, though.

A little bit of uneasiness kept giving her moments of
pause, too. Her talk with Lucy had gone well. Right?
Lucy seemed relieved that Jo had verified Rod's insistence that there was nothing to be found in the area
where the teen parties had been held. But…had Jo really convinced her sister? What was it Lucy said?

You think he imagined it, don't you?

Jo remembered what she'd said, too, suggesting the
friend had been both drunk and spooked by the cave.

Lucy hadn't exactly reacted, but she also hadn't said, "I'm sure you're right." Instead, she'd sounded troubled.

Except he wasn't that drunk. He was totally freaked out.

In retrospect, Jo realized that Lucy had been pushing back. Saying, *Jesse isn't like that.*

Yes, but Lucy had also admitted she had no desire herself to go wandering on her own off the beaten track in the cave. Hosting the party would have been different; she could be the knowledgeable one, the hostess who could offer something that would awe her friends. She wouldn't have been *alone.*

Midafternoon, Jo's own phone vibrated in her pocket, startling her. She was behind the cash register, but between customers, so she took it out. The number wasn't familiar, the area code one she didn't remember seeing before.

"Hello?" she said cautiously.

"Jo? This is Alan Burke."

She turned her head, seeing nobody within earshot and grateful for the momentary isolation. "Hi. Did everything go okay yesterday?"

"Yes, but we had to raise the second car this morning. No bodies," he said, as if reading her mind.

"Oh." Jo tried to think of something brilliant to say.

In that gritty voice, Alan said, "It's too late today, but... I wondered if you could get away to meet me for lunch tomorrow."

Warmth blossomed in her chest. "I...yes. I forgot to

do an errand the other day, so I need to get into town anyway."

"Café again? Or do you have another suggestion?"

"I hardly ever eat out when I'm home, so no. The café is fine."

They agreed on a time, and he disconnected. It was probably just as well that she didn't have a chance to squeal like a teenage girl or start second-guessing her agreement given that her stay in the area—and, from what she'd heard, very likely his as well—was limited. A crowd descended on the cash register, everyone eager to express their amazement and ask questions and spend money.

By closing time, Jo was back to focusing on her sister. Lucy was quiet at dinner, but not in a sulky way. Brody insisted on pushing his idea for a "wild cave" tour while they were eating.

"Two guys asked me today." He ignored the scowl on his father's face. "They thought we'd get a lot of people who are interesting in caving but want to try it out in a completely safe environment."

"Who said it would be completely safe?"

"It would be if we made the run over and over until we're confident," Brody argued.

"I said no. I meant no."

Brody's mouth opened as he prepared to push, but his gaze intersected Jo's. His jaw snapped shut and after a moment he bent his head to his meal.

Nobody had much to say after that. Another fun Summerlin family dinner. Playing peacekeeper had never been Jo's ambition in life. She hated conflict...

but of course she felt compelled to shield her siblings from their father's irritable stubbornness.

As Lucy rinsed plates and loaded the dishwasher, she said, "I wish Dad would go out. I can't even turn the TV on without him complaining it's too loud."

"He loans you his car, doesn't he, if you want to go hang out with friends?"

"I practically have to *beg*. And the last time I asked, he said, 'Remember what happened to Amy when *she* was driving around by herself.'"

Well, Rod did have a point, even if the way he treated Brody versus Jo and Lucy had always been noticeably different.

Lucy continued in a tone of discontent, "Anyway, Jaelin and Autumn are both working most evenings. Jaelin at the diner, and Autumn at Domino's Pizza. They're my two best friends."

That was particularly inconvenient. At Lucy's age, Jo had had a couple of friends who'd been lifesavers for her.

Wrinkling her nose as she scraped leftovers into a plastic bowl, she said, "I'd rather have your summer job than theirs."

"You *do* have the same summer job as me."

They both laughed.

"I can finish up if you want," Jo offered.

"Really? Thanks." Lucy vanished with haste that amused Jo, leaving her to wipe down counters and dry pans.

Oh, well. Brody had been doing his share. It wasn't as if Jo was eager to get to anything in particular.

She thought she heard Rod going out, but not the sound of a car engine, so Brody was probably still home. Once done, she debated turning on the TV herself—she could surely find something on the one streaming service Rod subscribed to—but decided she liked the quiet. She'd start a new book instead.

After closing the last cupboard, she headed for the stairs and started up just in time to see Rod walking down the hall up above. He wouldn't be going to bed yet, would he?

She was halfway upstairs when he opened his bedroom door. His bellow made her cringe.

"What the hell are you doing in my room, young lady?"

Oh, Lord—Jo had a bad feeling she knew exactly what Lucy was doing in her dad's bedroom.

When an all-out fight erupted, Jo hovered where she was, afraid she couldn't get to her own room unobserved but not wanting to be part of this, either. Lucy must have known the consequences if she got caught.

"I wouldn't have to sneak around if you didn't treat me like a baby—!" Lucy yelled.

"I can't trust you for a minute."

Rod was mad, and understandably so, Jo thought, cringing because *she* had committed the same sin just days ago. Still, Lucy hadn't exactly been demonstrating maturity lately, and he ought to be able to trust both his kids not to dig through his drawers and closet.

Jo crossed her fingers and prayed that her little sister didn't scream back that Jo had already found the hidden keys, so why didn't he go yell at her, too?

Maybe her having done that wasn't smart. Except

she truly had believed Lucy needed some reassurance, and that Rod would have said no. Hell, no.

The yelling went on. Brody's door briefly opened then closed. Not blaming him for his cowardice, Jo tiptoed to her own bedroom and sneaked inside, apparently unseen. Not that she couldn't still hear every word, solid wood doors or not. Lucy did not, as far as she could tell, betray Jo. But when the shouting went on and on, Jo finally stuck her head out in the hall just in time to hear Rod yelling, "Two weeks restriction!"

Jo cut in before Lucy could open her mouth again. "Enough already."

Rod turned his glare on her. "Butt out."

She raised her eyebrows. "Who called whom for help?"

He ground his teeth before leveling a stare at Lucy, already quivering in outrage.

"Forget two weeks! You're on restriction until you leave for college! Do you hear me?"

All Jo had wanted was peace and quiet so she could read the fantasy novel she'd picked out. The murder mysteries she usually enjoyed didn't have the usual appeal, not after these past few days.

Lucy screamed something unintelligible and ran into her room, slamming her bedroom door so hard the framed picture hanging in Jo's bedroom shook and ended up crooked despite the solidity of the walls in this old house. Rod stomped down the stairs almost loud enough to shake the house some more.

Jo couldn't call the ensuing quiet any more peaceful than were her thoughts.

ALAN LURCHED TO a sitting position as he emerged from a familiar but newly twisted nightmare, his shout still ringing in the room. God damn. He gave his head a hard shake. What was that about? Was his subconscious trying to tell him that a SEAL teammate had betrayed him? No. No. He'd never believe that. But somewhere in his head, a voice whispered, *How can you be so sure? After losing hostages because his fellow police officers either didn't follow orders or were unwilling to risk getting shot themselves, how can you believe in the* absolute *integrity of* anyone?

Swearing under his breath as he dug his fingers into his sweaty hair, Alan argued with himself. He had trusted his SEAL teammates. That's why it was so hard to know he might never find that kind of tight relationship again.

Chapter Nine

Alan bent to slam his tailgate to secure his latest purchase of a load of lumber, plumbing supplies and miscellany like new electrical outlet boxes, nodded his thanks to the gawky kid working for the lumberyard, then hopped down from the loading dock. He hoped this was a summer job for a boy in high school. Otherwise, his age radar must be seriously out of whack.

Shaking his head, he opened the door to jump in, but cocked his head when he heard an angry shout. It was followed by others. Curiosity led him to the alley, where he saw the small crowd partway down. Four men surrounding one, who was rotating slowly in place to keep an eye on all his potential assailants.

Didn't look like a fair fight to Alan.

He jogged that way.

"You moved here just before Christy was snatched," one of the guys yelled. "We don't get that many newcomers."

"I hadn't even heard the name until this week," protested the target.

Different voice. "*I* hear you asked her out. What happened, she say no?"

Oh, hell. Alan increased his pace to a run.

"What's going on here?" he asked as he reached the group.

All four spun to face him. His eyes briefly met those of the guy in the center, who appeared on edge but not in a panic. Good.

"None of your damn business," one of the would-be vigilantes snarled. "We just got things to say to Ryan here."

Ryan held himself tall, weight balanced on the balls of his feet, hands fisted. He wouldn't take what was coming lying down. And, damn it, Alan knew he'd seen him before. The picture formed in his head. Wearing a uniform. The youngest sheriff's department deputy, that's who he was.

Alan said calmly, "You have any real reason to think Deputy—" It came to him, because he'd known someone well with the same last name. "—Meehan ever knew Christy Dodswell?"

"He moved here not a month before she was grabbed," one of the bellicose twenty-something thugs snapped. "Gotta think what changed around here. And here it is. Meehan showed up."

"So you know everyone who moved into not only Mayville, but the surrounding counties? Victims have come from at least three counties, haven't they? Including Christy."

They all stared at him.

"What did you plan? To beat the snot out of Ryan

because he happened to be new in these parts when the first victim we know of—" Alan leaned heavily on that part "—disappeared?"

"What d'ye mean, *know of*?"

"I suppose you've all heard my name."

A few sullen bobs of the head.

"Why should we believe you were a SEAL?" one of them asked with a belligerent tilt to his chin.

Alan let his eyebrows climb. "Don't care what you believe. What's important here is that I was a police detective in a good-sized city for several years. This investigation isn't mine, but I have the experience to tell you the chances are good there are more victims than have been named. How hard would it be to grab a young woman who was just passing through town, maybe got a flat tire?"

"There were only two cars," mumbled the bulky guy Alan had begun to see as the ringleader.

"There are a lot of bodies of water around here, you know."

He saw on their faces that they knew.

"Runaways, hitchhikers, young women everyone assumes took off on their own. The four victims we believe are linked? They're probably the tip of the iceberg."

The four thugs were visibly thinking. That was something.

Alan added softly, "You do realize how much trouble you'd be in if you laid a hand on Deputy Meehan, don't you? Assaulting a law enforcement officer is a serious crime."

"We got a right to get answers."

Yep. Ringleader.

"You think of going to the police station and asking to talk to the primary investigator? Or Deputy Frazier, who led the searches?"

Some feet shuffled. Two of the men were looking at the ground now.

"If you have information that would point this investigation at anyone in particular—" Alan let his gaze rest on the young deputy "—either Detective Jantz or Deputy Frazier would be glad to hear it." He let his voice harden. "On the other hand, if all you have is a list of men in the area who might have moved here in a time range your limited knowledge tells you is suggestive, I'm thinking you'd be smart to go home and pretend this never happened."

Still in an ugly tone, the ringleader began, "We don't have to let—" Seeing that his compatriots were fleeing, he said, "We'll take this up another time."

"That had better be hot air," Alan called after him.

The jerk flipped him off behind his back.

Alan grunted.

Ryan Meehan, sweating only a little, grinned at him. "Thank you for your timely intervention."

Alan smiled and held out a hand. "Something tells me their plans wouldn't have gone well once they tried to take you on."

They shook. Meehan said, "Oh, they'd have made me sorry, but they would have been, too. I know them all. I've ticketed two of them and arrested a third one for assault in a brawl down at the Roundup."

"I'm not surprised. You on your way into work?"

Looking rueful, the young deputy said, "I dodged down the alley to avoid them. I was actually aiming for the lumberyard."

"Where I'm parked."

They walked the short distance together, continuing to talk. Meehan was relatively new in Mayville, but had grown up in Carthage, only a few counties away, so he wasn't exactly a stranger to these parts.

He grinned once more. "This job keeps me close enough I can get home for an occasional Sunday dinner, far enough away nobody in the family expects me to drop everything and run over when they need a handyman or hear a bump in the night."

Alan laughed, understanding on one level even though he'd never experienced that kind of family. "You plan to report this?" he asked, opening his truck door again.

Meehan went grim. "Damn straight. I might not bother, except… I can't be the only newcomer in the right time frame."

"No." Alan waved away more thanks and hopped in to drive the three blocks to the café.

Jo beat Alan to the diner, which surprised her. She suspected he always liked to be there to set up, whatever the situation. She did ask for the booth in back again, although took the side facing the front door. When she saw him walk in a couple of minutes later and their eyes met, she slid out and into the side that meant her back was to the door. Then she drank in the intensity in his unwavering stare and the sight of his tall, powerful body.

"You didn't have to do that," he said, when he sat down.

"No?"

"But thank you. I like to see what's coming."

"Surely nothing that alarming when there's probably not a man in town who would have the nerve to come after you."

"Call it habit." He reached for the menu but didn't start perusing it. "Anyway, you're presupposing anyone who came after me has any brains."

Jo chuckled. "You're right. How silly of me."

He flashed the grin that altered his face so drastically, deepening lines between his nose and mouth, making his eyes glint.

"I just came from a little standoff," he told her. "A few of the local geniuses had decided a guy who moved to town just before Christy Dodswell disappeared had to be the killer. It was four to one."

Hiding a spurt of worry, Jo studied him anew. "You don't look as if you've so much as bruised your knuckles."

"Nope. I talked some sense into them, although God knows how long that'll stick." He smiled past her, even before she realized their waitress was approaching.

Both ordered. He never had glanced at the menu, which meant he'd eaten here more than the once when she'd seen him.

"That's your pickup loaded with lumber out there?"

she asked, even though she knew it was. Who else had Virginia plates on a shiny black Ford F-150?

"Yeah, I'm going to tear down the detached garage and build a new one. Seems like a good time to do it. I'll need to have the trusses and what have you delivered, but I can start with the framing. At least around here I don't have to worry about rain."

"Bank says it's eighty degrees right now," she said. "You have more chance of getting burned to a crisp."

"Not me, but you would." He studied her. "I don't suppose you tan easily."

"Or at all." She wrinkled her nose. "I'm tempted to buy stock in a few suntan lotion companies."

That rusty laugh seemed to come more easily than it had the first time she'd heard it. And she was too pleased, given that there was no chance of starting anything with this man. In fact—their last two meetings had ended with him being a jerk.

She frowned. "So what's the deal with this? Are you planning to issue some bad news? A few warnings to mind my own business?"

His mouth tilted slightly. "Neither."

"Then…"

"I wanted to see you."

The few words spoken in a soft, gravelly voice hit her hard.

"I…"

He seemed to don a mask, in that way he had. "If I misled you, you don't have to stay."

That might be real indifference—but Jo didn't believe it. He was as attracted to her as she was to him, even though she couldn't imagine why.

A swallow unstuck her throat. "No. I wanted to see you, too."

Without any obvious movement, he relaxed in a way she couldn't miss. He nodded and said, "How's it going out there?"

Jo blinked. "Home? The cavern?"

"Both."

"Oh…home is tense. Did I tell you I'm here for the summer because of my teenage sister's rebellious behavior?" Well, of course she hadn't, although he seemed to know more about Brody than she'd expect.

"Someone mentioned you have both a sister and brother."

She made a face. "Lucy is sixteen and acting like she's thirteen. She and her dad are going at it, teeth and claws. I'm supposed to figure out why she's so worked up and fix her."

"*Her* dad?"

"My stepfather," she said uncomfortably. "I mostly call him by his name. Rod."

"You're not close?"

Their meals arrived, giving her a moment to realize she didn't know Alan Burke nearly well enough to be completely honest.

"Rod and I have an okay relationship," she said as she spread the napkin on her lap. "He's been good to me."

Alan hadn't moved, and his gaze seemed to see right

through her surface explanation. "That sounds less than wholehearted."

"As Lucy would say, Rod is all about the cavern. He started me working in the gift shop when I was twelve, and I was giving tours not that much later. Growing up, I felt like an employee more than a daughter." Strange. She'd never acknowledged that to herself before. She shrugged carelessly, as much for her benefit as for his. "He's sexist besides. *Brody* will inherit the great Summerlin Cavern, not Lucy. That's always been clear."

Alan had started in on his burger, but now he paused. "And not Jo," he said slowly.

"That was never a question." She picked up her own sandwich. "I wouldn't want it, anyway. As Lucy and I agreed the other day, there are worse part-time and summer jobs, though."

Alan smiled, as she'd hoped, but he didn't let the subject of her sister drop. "Have you had any breakthroughs with Lucy yet?"

Jo laughed. "Anyone who can ever claim to have broken through with a teenager is either a certifiable miracle worker or delusional."

His chuckle was more of a rumble. If she was able to rest her hand on his chest, she would feel the vibration. And even the thought was enough to make her cheeks warm.

The corners of his eyes crinkled, letting her know he'd seen the direction of her thinking, but all he said was, "What about Brody? How does he feel about being the anointed heir?"

"He's all about the cavern, too. I talked him into

going away to college, but he just let me know he thinks it was a waste of his time. Since his future is running the family business, he can learn more here than he can in any classroom."

"Where'd he go?"

She stiffened but told him.

"Springfield." Alan sounded thoughtful. "Not so far from home."

"Why are you so determined to suspect him?"

He wiped his fingers on the napkin and reached for a fry. "I'm not. I don't know him, but I think he's too young."

Relief filled her. "Of course he is. But you implied—"

"That Detective Jantz might want to talk to him? He probably will, if only because Brody knew the most recent victim well. If he has no ties to any of the other missing women—"

"I'm sure he doesn't." Okay, that had sounded too hasty. "He sticks close to home," she added.

"It's not that far a drive between the homes of any of the missing women," Alan pointed out.

"No, but—" But what? She shut her mouth, then opened it again. "Why are we talking about *my* family?"

"Because I don't have one."

"You told me that. I'm sorry. I'm...just being prickly."

That keen gaze made her feel as impenetrable as tissue paper. "Protective," he corrected her, sounding gentle. "I like that in a woman."

Oh, she understood that, more than she'd admit to anyone. Her mother had cast her off without a second thought. Alan's mother couldn't have been any prize, but at least she'd cared enough to remove him from his abusive home. No wonder he'd rank that quality high on his list.

Jo nodded, and they ate in silence for a few minutes.

When that began to feel awkward, she asked, "Are you planning to stay around here?"

He didn't jump to answer, but finally said, "I don't think so."

Jo eyed him. "Not so sure?"

His mouth twisted. "In the short term, my goal is to get the house and property in shape to sell. And no, probably not to your stepfather. His pressure has begun to irritate me. Beyond that… I don't know."

She wanted to ask what had happened to leave him at such loose ends, but knew that was getting too personal. Two casual lunches did not add up to a deep relationship. Maybe part of the attraction on both their sides was the fact that they were outsiders even if they had roots here in southern Missouri. Were his feelings as disturbed as hers?

An idea struck her that she hated, but it was a good one. She could settle at least part of her recent uneasiness.

"I was thinking," she said.

He leaned back in the booth and waited. Jo bet he was good at interrogation, patient enough to outwait just about anyone.

"This sounds weird, but part of Rod and my sister's recent dispute is because he's refusing to let her or Brody back in any of the cavern offshoots. The two passages off the tourist route are gated and locked."

Alan nodded, his eyes not leaving her face. "Wouldn't want those tourists wandering away."

"No. There was a time we all did a little exploring, usually with Rod. I think what happened was that Brody and Lucy both violated his trust this year by having parties for their friends back in a room in a closed-off passage."

"That would do it."

"Yes, but—" Tell him, or not? He had been a cop, and she didn't want to awaken those instincts. Still, she remembered the day she'd slipped through that gate and wished he was with her. Jo took a deep breath. "One of my sister's friends wandered away from the group and swears he saw a human skull."

"What?"

"You heard me. This wasn't that long ago. Like a month? Anyway, Rod was mad at Lucy and Brody both once he found out about the parties, but I think he actually hoped *he'd* find the skull, too. A mystery would go over well with tourists. That's if the skull really exists, I mean."

Oh, she had Alan's attention now, and wasn't sure she hadn't made a big mistake.

"Rod went back to try to find it, even though he was sure the friend was drunk and imagining things."

"That does seem the likeliest explanation," Alan commented. "Is your stepfather the only one who has looked?"

"No, he took a deputy with him, mostly to reassure

Lucy, I think. Deputy Hudson, the one who led one group of searchers."

Alan nodded.

"Of course they didn't find a thing. After that, Rod started hiding the keys so Brody and Lucy couldn't get back in there at all." She hesitated, but once again Alan waited her out. "Lucy was still so upset about it, claiming her friend wasn't that drunk and was really freaked by what he'd seen, that I…well, I found the keys and went looking, too."

"Good God."

To her astonishment, he reached across the table and closed his big warm hand around her much smaller one, probably because she'd been fidgeting.

"I couldn't find anything, either, but I had a tight window for my search. I sneaked in while a tour was going on." She took a deep breath. "Last night, Rod caught Lucy in his bedroom trying to find those blasted keys. He threw a fit."

"Did you rush to the rescue?" Was that a flicker of humor in his eyes?

She wrinkled her nose. "I hid in my bedroom. I think Brody did, too."

Alan chuckled again. "Smart."

"Yes, but—I realized there's a way I could get back in and take my time searching. Just to be sure."

"Why aren't you sure?" The question was so sharp, it felt like a knife slipping between her ribs.

The question scared her because she didn't like the real answer: How could it be coincidental that a human skull had been found during the same time span as a serial killer abducted women so nearby?

What she *said* was, "Because Rusty—our dog, remember?—was apparently with that boy when he claims to have seen the skull. He wandered away from the group because he heard Rusty barking and wondered why. So it's possible…"

"That the dog carried the skull away." Alan was thinking.

"Yes."

"So what's your great plan?"

She squared her shoulders and tipped up her chin. "I want your permission to enter the cavern from your property."

"You want to blunder in, try to navigate through a maze that covers as much as a couple of miles, in search of what might be a drunken kid's imaginary skull."

"I don't blunder," she said stiffly. "I do have experience, you know."

"You could have been knocked out the other day. My answer is no." He let go of her hand and lifted his to signal the waitress. "Are you finished?"

"You're being unreasonable… But yes. I lost my appetite."

"You're willing to take a substantial risk in an attempt to appease a teenager who might have let her imagination get the best of her." Any hint of warmth or understanding had evaporated. All she saw was the impassive man she'd first met. "No."

He took the bill from the waitress Jo had once again

failed to hear approaching, scanned it and pulled out his wallet.

He tossed some cash down and slid out of the booth, waiting while she did the same.

"Why won't—"

"Drop it." Out on the sidewalk, he gave a last curt nod and walked away, leaving her steaming behind him, but also failing to understand why he was both adamant and mad.

Chapter Ten

Alan thumped his forehead against the steering wheel in his truck. He'd screwed that one up, hadn't he? Usually, he was pretty good at talking people out of bad ideas—like, say, beating a sheriff's deputy.

After a minute, he pulled himself together enough to start the truck and pulled out onto the main street in town.

Not until, fifteen minutes later, he had turned into his own rough driveway did he identify the reason Jo's request was a trip wire for him. He'd believed she'd agreed to have lunch with him to get to know him. Because she felt this same, powerful draw. Had she thought she had to soften him up before she asked? Finding out she'd accepted his invitation because she wanted something from him, that offended him.

No, that hurt his feelings. So of course he'd lashed out at her, in his ice-cold version of a temper.

He backed up to his garage to make unloading easier, set the brake and turned off the engine, but continued to sit there, staring at the woods that climbed the slope. He'd barely known he *had* feelings that could be hurt, it had been so long since he had even tiptoed close to loving any one person. He might have been sensitized by learning that the people in his former police department he'd come to trust so readily let down the citizens they were hired to protect. Sure, it had been only a few officers, but the unnecessary deaths of innocents rankled until he found himself doubting anyone he was partnered with. The after-the-fact excuses told him those particular officers would be no more reliable on the next high-risk operation, because they were unwilling to accept responsibility and learn from mistakes.

Hell, maybe he'd just been naive, in a way. As a SEAL, he had never once questioned whether he could depend on his teammates or officers. A man got spoiled. In signing on with a police department, he'd thought he would find the same sense of honor and camaraderie.

Truth was, he'd been feeling unrooted ever since he walked away from the Richmond PD. Had he latched onto this attraction to Jo Summerlin out of sheer loneliness?

Maybe.

Irritated at himself, he hopped out and started unloading. As he dropped a bag of nails onto the concrete floor of the garage, a faint smile touched his mouth. He could be wrong about Jo's reasons for having lunch with him, but he felt very sure that he hadn't heard the last of her determination to burrow into the earth from his property. If that wasn't a mulish woman, he'd never met one.

Pausing in the act of heaving a pile of two-by-fours

to his shoulder, he wondered if she *would* bother asking again. After all, she'd tell herself, what was he going to do? Have her thrown into jail if he found out after the fact that she'd sneaked into the cavern opening despite his refusal?

If he were being pushed the same way, wasn't shrugging and going ahead despite obstacles exactly what he'd do?

This smile was crooked.

It died slowly when he started to wonder exactly why she was so determined. She was afraid for someone in her family—or was she afraid of what one of them might have done?

And why would that have even crossed her mind?

Jo CROUCHED AT the edge of the woods, dismayed at how much open ground lay between her and the much smaller half-moon opening to the cavern that she remembered from the time Rod had brought her and Brody to explore, back after Alan's father had died and the property was deserted. It appeared Alan had cleared a large swath of land that had been overgrown then. What was left was too stubbly to qualify as lawn, but he'd certainly be able to see anyone crossing his property if he happened to be looking.

This early in the morning, it appeared he hadn't yet come out to start work on the garage. He'd already knocked down part of the original structure, but still had a way to go before he could build anew on the concrete pad. His pickup was parked in front of the half-destroyed garage; a pile of lumber lay to one side. She didn't see any movement behind the windows in the house. He wouldn't still be asleep, would he? If only she could be that lucky.

She hesitated and did some more reconnoitering. She could skirt around a stretch of the open land while staying in the cover of the woods, but not very far. Since the cavern entrance was on the opposite side of Alan's house from the garage, if he did happen to pop out to start work, the house might hide her during her quick dash.

Unless she was going to turn around and go back, she had zero choice—and she didn't want to do that. The tension in the Summerlin house last evening had been awful. Lucy had come down to dinner, but her eyes had barely been visible behind red swelling. Jo didn't consider her chastened, though; if the set of a mouth could be considered mutinous, Lucy's was. Hardly anyone said a word. Rod glowered, snarled and shoveled in his food. Brody kept his head down and did likewise. Lucy stirred the food around on her plate. Jo had picked at hers.

After dinner, Brody had cornered her in the kitchen. "Just so you know," he said in a low voice after a cautious glance toward the living room, "Dad caught Lucy in his truck, digging in the glove compartment and under the seats."

Jo had moaned. "Did she find the keys?"

"I don't think so, but… What is she *thinking*?"

Jo truly didn't know. There had to be more to this

than teenage resentment because her own father didn't believe her. Jo worried at being in the dark about her sister's real fear.

Now, stumbling over a broken branch, Jo grimaced because that might be a lie. *She* wasn't going to all this effort to prove that there was a two-hundred-year-old skeleton tucked back there somewhere in the Summerlin Cavern. If that was true, Rod would have found it. He had every motivation in the world.

What she couldn't get away from was the timing of all this. The juxtaposition of Lucy's friend finding something like that and the disappearance of all those women. Jo didn't want to believe there was any connection between those murders and her family…but a sense of creeping uneasiness stayed with her. The horrible thing was, if a killer was using the cavern, there were only a few possible suspects: Brody; Austin, who constantly hit on women and maybe didn't accept a no as well as she'd thought he did; and Rod, who looked on women with disrespect, possibly including his own daughter and his stepdaughter.

Rod, who returned to the cavern nearly every evening and stayed for hours.

How could anyone else have secretly slipped into the cavern for years?

She could forget all about this awful suspicion if only she could successfully sneak in by this back route, navigate her way to recognizable passages, and be absolutely sure nothing as nasty as she was imagining could have taken place there. Right this minute, she kicked herself for not extending her search the day she'd gone looking. People would have wondered at her absence, but she could have lingered through the cycle until another tour had just set out.

Anyone could have been using this end of the cave to stash victims all these years, given that the property had been deserted. Alan's father had used it to hide his meth lab, from what she'd heard. Other criminals had taken advantage of the state's extensive cave system over the years. But if that were the case…how could a skull have showed up so far away from this opening? What had upset Rusty so much the night Amy disappeared?

Jo moaned. Her mind had been spinning in circles all night. A headache was only one result.

She stopped, clutching a leafy branch in front of her while she scanned again for any movement, then took a deep breath and sidled into the open. When nothing happened, she broke into a run, her small pack bouncing on her back.

Jo went all out. She was fast if she didn't have to run too far. No shout interrupted her race for the dark maw of the cave. Her breath came hard. Almost there. Almost there. Only yards from her goal…

A man stooped to avoid hitting his head and stepped out of the cave opening right in front of her, planted his feet and crossed his arms.

Alan had been waiting for her. His expression was implacable.

Furious and embarrassed, Jo came to a stop.

"How DID YOU KNOW?" were the first words out of her mouth.

Alan couldn't decide if he was most annoyed or gratified that he'd read her right.

"Wasn't hard to tell no wasn't the answer you wanted," he said.

Puffing from the all-out dash, she glared at him. "Why would you care if I do this? I've been through all the way to our end before."

He didn't move. "And how long ago was that?"

"It was…" She opened and closed her mouth a few times. "Ten—no, maybe eleven or twelve years ago?"

Alan shook his head. "You did it by yourself?"

Her cheeks were already red, but he thought she also blushed. "No. Rod and Brody and I did."

"Your father wasn't setting a very good example for you, was he?"

"Stepfather," Jo said sharply.

She really didn't want to own Rod Summerlin, Alan noted. More had to be going on there than she'd let him see.

"This is a bad idea," he told her. "What kind of equipment did you bring?"

Chin jutted, she said, "A helmet. A couple of lights. Pads to protect my knees and arms. Water, snacks. Markers."

"A rope?"

"No, we're on the same level."

He shook his head. "Last time, you trailed behind an expert. Today, you're inadequately equipped for anything to go wrong. Did you even tell a soul what you had in mind, in case you got lost or injured?"

She glared at him.

"Didn't think so. Would you recommend anyone else head in there alone? Without having left word of where they were going?" He jerked his head toward the dark, cool opening behind him.

Did she sag? "You know I wouldn't," she mumbled.

He discovered that he hated the look of near desperation in Jo's eyes. This was no mere impulse, he realized. And yeah, she'd volunteered to accompany him into that cave they'd found during their search, but he hadn't seen any indication that she was exhilarated by the potential challenge. Excitement was the last thing she was feeling now. She thought she *had* to do this.

"Jo, you need to tell me what this is about."

"I did! Lucy's friend found—"

Alan shook his head. "There's more to it." If he sounded harsh, he couldn't help himself. Whatever this was had to connect to those missing women. He couldn't think of anything else that would explain her anxiety. Especially given that Jo's family had the best access to the cavern.

Except maybe for any long-term employees, he amended. He needed to look into that.

She still had her lips pressed together, and he still hated the darkness in her eyes.

He couldn't stop himself from taking a step closer to her and lightly squeezing her upper arms. "You're scared," he said, gentle now. "Why?"

"Why should I tell you?"

Alan hadn't even realized he'd made the decision, but he answered right away. "Because if you do and I agree that this needs doing, I'll consider going with you."

Hope filled her eyes along with a sheen of tears.

"Damn it," he growled, and kissed her.

Shocked at himself, he started to lift his head. But Jo had made a tiny whimpering sound and pushed up on her toes to resume the kiss. He nipped her lower lip sharply and took advantage of her gasp to slide his tongue into her mouth.

God, she tasted good. When he pulled her up tight to his body, she felt even better—slim, supple, feminine. Her fingers bit into his neck as she held on and kissed him back. His thinking blurred and he might have surrendered to the sheer pleasure if his arm wrapping her hadn't bumped into the backpack.

He groaned and tore his mouth away from hers. Voice rough, he asked, "Are you trying to sway me into letting you go ahead?"

She stared at him dazedly, as if it took her a few seconds to parse his words. Then she whispered, "Can I?"

His hands tightened on her. "Probably."

She breathed out an "o-oh." The sound was almost as sexy as her earlier whimper.

"Damn." Alan made himself release her. "You need to be honest with me."

Deep reluctance showed on her fine-boned face, but then she took a deep breath. "I…it's just that I'm probably crazy even to be thinking what I have been. It's nothing but little things added up. Nothing solid."

"I can guess some of it." He backed up enough to keep himself from touching her again. He didn't like thinking that she'd responded to his kiss with such passion for exactly the reason he'd suspected. "Is this an emergency?"

"No! I mean, not that I know. It's one more place to look, that's all."

Hadn't it occurred to her that the man who had been abducting these women might not be killing them right away? That he might hold them for awhile to enjoy them? That Amy Kendall might still be alive?

He almost shook his head. What were the odds of that? She'd disappeared—what?—nine or ten days ago? From the perspective of the killer, it was bad enough that the cops and general public hadn't bought the "she must have taken off on her own" explanation, that they'd mounted searches. Even if she'd still been alive, the news that her car had been found had probably signed her death warrant. That had to have shaken the killer.

And really, the idea that victims had been held in the Summerlin Cavern, one of the state of Missouri's best-known show caves, one toured by hundreds of people every single day at this time of year, many thousands a year, stretched credulity. He wanted to know why Jo thought it was a realistic possibility.

"Talk to me," he said.

A spark of defiance resurfaced. "If you decide I am out of my mind, are you going to keep saying no?"

Deciding, Alan shook his head. "You need to do this. We'll do it together, but not until tomorrow morning. I need time to put together the equipment we should carry, and Drew Frazier and a couple of his friends are due here in about an hour to help me finish taking down the garage and starting to frame the new building."

She nodded and they walked back to his house. No, she didn't want a drink, so they sat on the porch steps in the sunlight that hadn't yet become blistering, and she talked.

Jo KNEW SHE really hadn't used her head. Thank goodness Alan had stopped her! If nothing else, taking off without giving Rod a chance to find a substitute for her had been a crummy thing to do.

Plus, instead of telling anyone where she was going, she'd relied on Alan guessing what she'd done if he heard she was missing. Not smart. What if he'd taken off somewhere for a few days? Worked on his place and didn't hear for ages that she was missing?

Jo had never thought of herself as reckless, but that's what her plan had been.

As it was, Alan had walked her back to her car, stashed in a leafy turnout half a mile toward town from his driveway. After giving it a sardonic look, he'd bent his head and kissed her, quick and hard, before saying, "Make it as early as you can slip away."

Thanks to him, to his promise to accompany her on her quixotic quest, not to mention his kisses, enough of her tension had diminished to leave her feeling she could act normal for the rest of the day.

Despite that kiss, she couldn't help wondering if

she'd damaged whatever was developing between them by her defiance of his direct refusal to let her access the cavern from his property. Or was the second kiss meant as reassurance? Jo couldn't tell. She did know he'd already been mad because she'd asked his permission when they met for lunch, although she had no idea why and hadn't wanted to ask.

She wouldn't tell him how hazy her memory was of how she, Rod and Brody had made it from the Burke end of the cave to the familiar passages on Summerlin land. She did remember dark, yawning alternative tunnels and cracks that might lead who knew where. Rod had seemed certain of the route, which in retrospect made her realize he'd taken it before. Maybe from the other end? Possibly repeatedly over the years. His frustration at not owning the whole thing had never dropped below a simmer, that was for sure, which made no sense to her. It had to be ego, because Rod already owned additional sections of the cavern that were show quality, if he wanted to expand.

Once Jo parked at the house, leaving her backpack in the trunk, she ran to the cavern and found Rod organizing a group of tourists. He stepped aside and snapped, "Where the hell have you been?"

"I'm so sorry. A good friend from college called. She's—her fiancé was killed in a car accident yesterday. I was going to let you know I needed a couple of days to attend their wedding in July."

Rod's expression changed. He was buying this, which induced an attack of guilt. He *had* been good to her.

These suspicions made her feel like a horrible human being.

Even so, she had to do this. She *had* to.

"She lives in Kansas City," Jo hurried on. "I promised I'd drive up there tomorrow, and...well, probably spend the night. Can you find someone to fill in for me? I'll leave first thing in the morning, and if she seems all right, come home as soon as possible."

"Yeah, I can do that."

It had to be her guilt at lying that made her think he was studying her with more care than usual.

"Tomorrow shouldn't be one of our busiest days," she offered.

Tuesdays were typically the slowest of the week.

"Yeah, yeah. You're here now. Can you take this group?" He jerked his head toward the cluster of people.

She forced a smile. "You bet."

In his usual way, he walked away without another word.

She made it through the rest of the day without anyone appearing to suspect that she was hiding any turmoil. At a slow moment, Austin and she talked for longer than usual, him actually asking what the deal was with Lucy and Rod.

Surprised he'd noticed, Jo made a face. "They've gone to war. That's really why I came home for the summer, you know. To step in as peacekeeper."

"Did something happen?" he asked, his puzzlement appearing genuine.

"Between them? If something incited all this, neither has told me," Jo lied. "You're always around. Haven't things been tense for a while?"

He wouldn't like knowing how his frown deepened wrinkles, adding years to his usually boyish face. "Not so's I noticed, but when she's in school, we don't see that much of her. You know."

"Weekends…"

He shrugged. "I don't pay that much attention. It's just lately—"

Yes, indeed. Who wouldn't notice Lucy's incinerating glares every time her and her father's paths crossed?

Of course, at the end of the day, Austin threw out a hopeful, "I don't suppose you'd like to get away from your family for a few hours?"

He took her polite refusal well. She thought.

Lucy refused to come down to dinner. The two men ate with their usual single-minded dedication. Jo wondered if she herself was losing weight, as little interest as she'd had lately in her meals. Without sharing his destination, Brody took off immediately in his noisy truck. What were the odds Lucy would bound down the stairs to cheerfully help clean the kitchen? Rod growled, "I have to get some work done," and went out the front door.

Jo felt as if she ought to check on Lucy, but her own stress level was plenty high without her sister dumping any more on her. A couple of hours later, voices drifted to her, making her aware that Lucy and Rod were going at it again, but since they were downstairs, she couldn't make out what they were actually saying.

Feet stamped up the stairs. Eventually, Jo heard

Brody on his way up at what her bleary eyes told her was almost two in the morning. Rod wouldn't be happy if Brody was hungover tomorrow.

She'd set her phone alarm for 5:00 a.m. The house was quiet when she dressed wearing several layers and grabbed her toiletries from the bathroom to support her pretense of a trip to Kansas City.

All three other bedroom doors were firmly closed. Ugh—she ought to peek in at Lucy before she left. Yet more guilt, because she really should have tried to talk to her last night?

Rather than knocking and waking everyone up, she eased the door open and quietly stepped in. Enough dawn light penetrated the blinds to allow her to see that her sister's bed was empty. Not just empty—clearly unslept in.

Oh, God. Had this latest fight been the last straw? Had Lucy taken off once everyone else had gone to bed? And…had she taken her dad's truck?

Jo sighed, knowing how furious that would make him. Better to hope Lucy had called a friend to come out and get her. Figuring out where she'd gone would have to wait until tonight. Jo had met several of Lucy's friends now, but probably not all. She didn't know most of their last names, and without Lucy's phone, didn't have numbers where she could contact them. Anyway, it wasn't as if she wanted to wake Rod and say, "Oh, by the way, your daughter took off last night without telling anyone, but she's okay and will be home when she feels like it."

She'd just hope Lucy came home or called her dad

this morning. Jo did take a moment to text her sister, hoping for a response before she and Alan plunged into the cavern and lost phone reception. She'd be happier to know where Lucy was.

Slipping out into the hall, she gently closed her sister's bedroom door to put off for as long as possible Rod noticing her absence.

Then she tiptoed down the stairs to make her own getaway.

Chapter Eleven

With the garage at Alan's place only a skeleton, Jo had no place to park her car where it wouldn't be seen by anyone coming up the driveway.

He'd emerged from the house and was waiting when she got out. "Something wrong?" he asked.

He had managed to look even more daunting than usual this morning, which was saying something. She hadn't expected him to be wearing a one-piece coverall of thin but tough nylon. He'd obviously done enough caving to have the kind of clothing that stood up best to conditions. Well-worn boots with impressive tread. She guessed he'd held on to his equipment from his days as a SEAL. Then, if he'd gone into a cave, he'd have wanted to pass unseen—thus the black coverall and black Wellington boots.

Jo wished she was anywhere near as well equipped. No wonder he'd looked askance at her yesterday.

Remembering his question, she said, "Oh, I was wishing my car was out of sight, but that's silly. There's no reason anyone would come looking for me here."

"Where do they think you went?"

She told him her cover story, and Alan nodded without comment. He looked...not grim, exactly, but purposeful. Without asking, he took her pack from her and rooted through it, then eyed her boots.

"We'll likely be doing some wading. I went to town yesterday and picked up a shell layer that should fit you. We can tape it over your boots to keep you mostly dry." He nodded at her feet. "Don't suppose you have neoprene booties under there?"

Chagrined, she said, "A couple of layers of wool socks. I don't remember having to get wet when we made this trip."

"What time of year was that?"

She tried to recall, but had no idea.

"Probably fall. Right now, we'll be wading some streams. Your socks should be fine, as long as we get boots and pants sealed. At least you brought an extra pair of socks."

Gee, she'd done something right. But she kept her mouth shut, because she was realizing what deep trouble she'd have been in if she had succeeded in setting out on her own yesterday.

She followed Alan to the house. The front porch, including roof, was obviously new, but the interior remained shabby. It looked like he was essentially camping in here, not trying to make the place homey.

She accepted the oversuit from him—yellow, probably all he could find—and said, "I'll pay you back for this."

He grunted. "Go put it on."

Both of them put on their helmets and strapped on knee pads before they left the porch. Her helmet was an old-time, battered one, probably manufactured for a miner, which didn't mean it wasn't perfectly fine. His, of course, she recognized as an ultralight one with a fancy lighting system. Way to make her feel inadequate, she thought wryly.

Ten minutes later, he led the way to the cave opening. Jo rustled in the extremely unflattering, loose-fitting suit she'd managed to get on over her jeans and layered shirts. Not that it mattered what she looked like, she lectured herself. A fleecy balaclava now circled her neck, uncomfortably warm given the time of year, but she knew it would help her maintain her body temperature once they were deep in the cavern, especially if she got wet. She'd be grateful to be able to pull it up.

She eyed the pack Alan had hefted so effortlessly and wondered what he was carrying. Getting the pack through any narrow places would be more of a squeeze than easing his big body through. The one obvious addition was a coil of rope and some carabiners hanging on the outside. Jo knew they'd stayed on one level during that long-ago adventure, but Alan was prepared if they couldn't for some reason, which was both alarming and reassuring.

He stopped in the opening and assessed her one more time. "You set?"

She nodded, striving for confidence. "Let's do it."

What she was really thinking was a fatalistic, *Let's get this over with.*

ALAN HAD VENTURED into the cavern only once since returning to Missouri a few months back. Then he hadn't
had to go far, and had had a specific purpose. Today,
he didn't need to hesitate when the passage split fifteen
minutes or so on their way. Deciding he'd rubbed in
his point well enough, he refrained from stopping and
asking, *So, which way?* He respected Jo's determination and didn't want to embarrass her.

He gestured for her to walk ahead, mostly so he
could more easily keep an eye on her. Their previous
experience had given him some faith in her ability to
make smart decisions rather than foolish mistakes, but
call him a skeptic: this was a more challenging trip,
and he intended to lead when the going got tougher.

If they'd been doing this for fun, he would have
taken her the other way, where eventually the remnants
of a number of different enterprises could be seen. If he
stayed around here long enough, he might clean it up;
none of it was picturesque, just gave a sense of local
history. Someone had tried some mining in here, God
knows what for, and left wooden shoring, oil cans, even
blasting cord. At a small pool, what had probably been
a summer house for keeping food cool still stood. And
last but most offensive was equipment left from his father's manufacturing of methamphetamine. Cleaning
that junk out had been the first task he'd set himself
after moving into the house. He'd been relieved not to
find any actual meth, although this was a big cavern
with a lot of nooks and crannies, and plenty could be
hiding from him. Still, he thought it likely that other
people, including some of his dad's customers, had

gone exploring in here after finding out about his death. If there'd been any product left, Alan believed it was long gone.

Initially the way he and Jo needed to take was open, the roof slanting down here and there but typically remaining high enough he didn't have to bend his head. Walls, ceiling and floor were rough. More debris was strewn on the floor than he recalled, but no more than you'd expect from natural changes. Caves were living, breathing entities in a way most people didn't understand. Change was slow and subtle, one drip of water at a time, but never-ending. Cave-ins, or the fall of a large stalactite to shatter below, happened, but given the miles of passages in this cavern alone, were a tiny part of the ongoing story.

He could have moved faster than Jo went, but liked that she stepped carefully. He didn't see her trip once in the first forty-five minutes or so. She stopped only one time, when the ceiling rose high above and the walls opened into a vast space bigger than any in the Summerlin Cavern that he'd seen. Drapery formations along one wall added to the drama. Jo let the beam of her light play across the spectacular folds that might have been heavy stage curtains hung from the ceiling. They shone a deep gold in the light.

"I remember this." It was the first thing she'd said since they set out. "Rod talked about what he could do with it." Wryness in her voice, she added, "It was going to waste, he said."

"Yeah? What would he do with it? Hold parties?"

Without turning his helmet light directly onto her

face, he couldn't be sure of her expression, but thought she grimaced.

"Probably hoard it," she mumbled. "Am I right in thinking we go that way?" She pointed.

Impressed, Alan inclined his head. She was right on, maybe a better navigator than he would have guessed.

Twenty minutes or so later, the narrowed passage opened again, this time into a space where there was no pretense of a flat floor. Limestone had worn smooth into slopes tilting this way and that. Fortunately, the one they had to ascend wasn't difficult to scramble up. From here, magnificent stalactites and stalagmites, some joined in vast columns, created the illusion of an ancient ruin carved out of the native rock like Petra in Jordan. Even the color wasn't dissimilar, although the sandstone in that part of the world was nearly a true rose color, while much of the cavern varied from pale gold to a vivid orange. Once, he'd been able to visit Petra when he'd been in that part of the world. Even then, he'd made mental comparisons with Missouri's magnificent underworld.

From here, a caver could have chosen any of eight or ten exits, although Alan knew from experience that some were dead ends. They varied from a crack like an ice crevasse to a large arched opening that could be reached only by rock climbing. Alan led Jo to a giant rift between slanting rock walls that in places had a walkable floor; other brief stretches required they use the technique of a rock climber maneuvering up a chimney, but here they inched along sideways. He had to take his pack off his back for the first time. He attached it to his belt with a stretchy cord and hauled it along behind him like an ungainly overweight pet.

When the crack was at its narrowest, he saw deep unhappiness on Jo's face. Not fear, exactly, but she wasn't having a good time. She was plenty strong enough to move confidently, bracing herself between the wall behind her and the wall in front of her, but he suspected she wouldn't have chosen to go on if she hadn't known the way soon opened into a more conventional cave passage.

"Ugh," she mumbled, when she dropped out of the rift next to him. Her knees momentarily buckled, and he put a hand around her elbow.

"You okay?"

"Sure," she said sturdily.

"Let's take a break," he suggested. "I could use a drink." Maybe, he realized, because for the first time he *heard* running water.

He found a place to sit where he could rest his back against a rock. Jo settled right beside him.

Both rummaged in their packs and came up with water bottles. He took out a packet of almonds, too, and offered some to her. Then he said, "Let's save on our lights," and turned his off. A moment later, she did the same. He blinked momentarily against afterimages, before he was left to stare blindly at the complete darkness.

Something skittered off to his right. Jo jumped.

"Probably a salamander," he said. "I saw one earlier."

She let out an audible breath. "I really don't mind the darkness. It just..."

"Triggers something primal in us," he suggested. "Hear that? It's probably a small waterfall."

"Oh! I hadn't noticed."

He liked her voice. He'd long since become aware of how much voices revealed in the absence of other sensory input. Hers was midrange, imbued with warmth that made him feel as if he'd just spread his hands over a campfire, stroked a purring cat, been wrapped in a woman's arms.

Where she was concerned, her arms wrapped tightly around him sounded good.

Some crunching ensued. After a minute, he asked, "Did you see any of your family this morning before you left?"

"I…no."

Alan zeroed in on that tiny break. The feeling something besides where to park had bothered her earlier.

"What?" he asked, then reached for her hand so he could pour some more almonds into her palm.

"Thanks." She went quiet for a minute. "My sister wasn't in her bed this morning. She either ran away or— No, probably just took off to spend the night with a friend. Rod will be mad, although I may be wrong in thinking she didn't tell him last night."

"She still determined to get back in the cavern?"

"More than ever." Worry vibrated in Jo's voice. "Brody says she looked for the keys in Rod's truck yesterday. Of course, he caught her. She doesn't have the making of a successful undercover agent."

No, the kid didn't, which worried him, too. Lucy's dramatics and blundering around wouldn't amount to much if Alan and Jo's foray today turned into a wild goose chase. But if there was anything real to Lucy's fears—and Jo's—that was another story. The girl could be endangering herself in a way she was too young— and too trusting of her family—to foresee.

His silence hadn't soothed Jo, who said suddenly, "Do you think she's all right?"

"You know she's most likely at a friend's, receiving the sympathy nobody gives her at home."

"*I* give her sympathy."

He didn't hear the indignant sniff, but one was there, and it made him smile, even though... Alan frowned. This expedition wasn't all for Jo's sake anymore. He'd developed his own case of disquiet. An itch—and he'd learned over the years to pay attention to those.

"Ready to move on?" he asked abruptly.

"Of course."

JO HOPED ALAN couldn't tell how much she hated the one truly tight "choke" they had to get through, a crack narrow enough she had to squirm, shifting one shoulder at a time, releasing all her air at the critical moment, feeling her breasts getting squished and scraped. She didn't remember it being anywhere near this bad, but of course she'd been a lot younger. Slight. She hadn't developed much until she was...oh, fourteen or fifteen, and then slowly.

How Alan would get through, given his greater size, she couldn't imagine. Once she was safely on the other side, he shoved her pack through, then opened his own and handed bulkier items through one at a time. The coil of rope came on its own, as did something squishy that she identified as a sleeping bag. Apparently he believed in taking all the precautions. Then the pack, which he was able to flatten now with only the smaller items still in it. Finally, she all but held her breath as he wedged himself into a space where a large man with his muscle mass couldn't possibly fit.

Somehow he did, easing inch by inch with a grace that told her he'd had plenty of practice in similar tight spots.

Once he was through, he shook himself. "That was easier when I was a kid."

Jo made a face. "I was thinking the same thing."

"I don't suppose you brought a key to the gate, so once we get there we can just let ourselves out instead of taking this trip in reverse."

"Don't I wish."

She sighed, pushed her arms through the straps of her pack and waited until Alan had repacked his and swung it to his back. Then they started out again, Alan having to stoop a little, her able to walk upright.

"Do you know how much longer this will take?" she asked after a minute. Why hadn't she asked him at the beginning?

He must be pondering, because he took his time before saying, "I'm guessing a couple more hours."

Oh, boy. Jo wished she'd brought more food. Seeing the big pack in front of her, though, she suspected Alan had plenty for both of them.

"Do you have a deadline?" he asked.

"No."

He was right about the wading. The next short waterfall they encountered tumbled into a stream that filled the entire passage. It wasn't deep, she saw, when he stepped into it with confidence, but the water was shin deep on him, almost knee-deep with her shorter stature.

"Grab my belt," he instructed her. "If you fall, you'll get soaked. Yell if I'm going too fast."

At least the current wasn't strong.

They stayed in the stream for what seemed forever, but realistically was probably no more than fifteen minutes. Jo didn't bother checking the time.

Another half hour or so along, she began to suspect that she would have gotten lost in here, sooner if not later. She'd planned to mark places when she had to choose one direction or another, so she'd eventually have been able to find her way back out, but the chances of her making it to the Summerlin Cavern end?

Zero, at least without taking all day. And think how much fun spending the night all by herself deep in the cavern would have been?

She stumbled to a stop when Alan did, and let his firm grip on her arm guide her a few steps. He gently eased her to sit on a flat-topped rock, swung his pack off and lowered himself beside her.

"We need to eat and take a rest."

Jo hoped he hadn't noticed that her legs had been shaking.

"Your feet dry?" he asked.

She wriggled her toes. "I think so."

"Good. I brought a couple of ham sandwiches. Does that sound okay?"

"Yes!" Her fervency embarrassed her. Another handful of nuts wouldn't cut it.

His low chuckle warmed her. Again, he turned out his light after he found what he wanted in his pack, and once he dug out his bottle of water, Jo did the same. She accepted a sandwich from him, the handover only slightly fumbled.

They ate in silence for a minute.

"You holding up all right?" he asked finally.

"You don't think I am?" Jo asked in alarm.

"Didn't say that. You're doing fine."

"Oh." She relaxed. "This is a lot longer trip than I remembered."

He made a humming sound.

"You must have done some caving when you were a SEAL."

The pause was brief. "I did. Several parts of the world. I conducted a few training sessions here and there, too. Not everyone had had the chance to go underground, depending on what part of the country they were from."

"No, that's true. Although there are caves in quite a few states."

The big shoulder touching hers moved in what she took as agreement.

When he made no attempt to keep talking, she decided to be bold. "Will you tell me why you quit your job to come home to Mayville?"

If he told her it was none of her business, she

wouldn't be surprised. Or, really, offended, because…
it wasn't. But he'd been open about his childhood, his
father's abuse and mother's determination to get him
away. So—

This silence had gone on long enough that she was
surprised when he said, "Once I was out of the navy, I
signed on as a cop. Did patrol for about a year, but my
specialized skills got me promoted fast. I…liked being
a detective. Said no thanks to SWAT."

"Would you have been able to do that if your injury
kept you out of remaining as a SEAL?"

"Not a hundred percent sure. Didn't want to find
out."

She felt his shrug. That contact, shoulders and upper
arms and thighs, anchored her. More, it made her very
aware of his body in a more visceral way than when
she watched him move.

He'd quit talking, and Jo didn't quite have the nerve
to demand he spit it out. For some reason, she felt sure
whatever had ended his career as a detective was a lot
more dramatic than *just thought I'd take some time off.*
The story was his to share, or not.

"I mostly liked and trusted the men I worked with."
Even in the dark, Jo could tell he'd turned his head as if
to look at her. "There were women in the department,
just none in my unit."

Jo nodded, however meaningless that was when he
couldn't see her.

"Two guys robbed a bank, shot and killed a loan officer and made it out with three hostages. A couple of
customers and a teller. I happened to be nearby. By the

time I got there, they'd fled into a ramshackle riverfront warehouse. Lots of possible exits. I didn't see that we dared wait half an hour or more for a SWAT team to arrive. They'd have been long gone. This…wasn't an unfamiliar exercise for me."

From his years as a SEAL, he meant.

Tension vibrated through him. Jo felt compelled to grope until she found his hand. He latched onto hers.

"My biggest fear was that they'd kill the hostages once they got to their escape vehicle. Why not, when they'd already killed? I grabbed another detective and two uniforms. They argued, but I made the mistake of thinking once we made a plan, I could depend on them to follow it." He shook his head. "It was a debacle."

"Oh, no," Jo whispered.

"The detective…never made it into position at all. One of the uniformed officers got excited and started firing, giving away his position and, oh yeah, killing a hostage. I took down the robbers, but by then they'd shot a second hostage. In the aftermath, my brass wasn't all that supportive even though while I was cuffing one of the robbers, two of us heard him talking about how much pleasure he'd have taken in throwing the hostages' bodies at us."

"They thought you should have waited?"

"Yeah. I keep asking myself the same question. I still think all three women would have been dead. What's more, it should have been a straightforward operation, four of us against two who were already panicking. As it was, nobody even pinned the detective down on where he'd vanished to. The one who started shooting

prematurely..." Alan shifted. "I imagine he'll be tor-
turing himself for a good long while, too."

"I'm sorry."

His fingers tightened on hers. "I lost a level of trust
and finally made the decision to quit. Don't know what
kind of recommendation I'll get if I try to get hired
with any other department. Don't know if I want to."

Hearing the desolation in his voice along with the
deep anger, Jo swiveled as far as she could and clum-
sily wrapped her arms around Alan. In close to a lunge,
he hauled her into a tight clinch.

If the position and the rough rock beneath her butt
hadn't been so uncomfortable, she'd have been happy
to stay where she was forever.

Especially once his mouth found hers.

Chapter Twelve

An hour later, Alan decided to call another halt. He'd been pressing on hard. Not like Jo wasn't fit, but not many people worked out as seriously as he did. She had to be beat, but she didn't say a word. Just stuck with him, did what she had to do, a quality he admired.

Why had he said so much to her? he asked himself.

Had he been testing Jo? he wondered. Wondering how far *she* trusted him and his judgment? Given how short a time they'd known each other, he shouldn't have put that kind of pressure on her. The way she'd reached for him, though, expressed a whole hell of a lot.

What he really shouldn't have done was kiss her even if he had hungered to do just that since the first time he'd succumbed to temptation where she was concerned. It wouldn't be so bad if this one had been just a kiss, but he'd call it a revelation instead. She'd fit perfectly in his arms, despite their awkward position. He loved her taste, the strength of her fingers digging into his neck and stroking his hair. And, damn, he'd have given just about anything to strip her and make love to her, then and there.

Sure, that would have been romantic.

He grimaced. Had she spoken a single word since he'd reluctantly released her? Why would she, when all he'd done was growl something like, "Bad time and place for this," which could be taken a lot of different ways.

It would help if he weren't so conflicted about this attraction, about whether he could imagine having a relationship with a sweet elementary school teacher. And, no, that wasn't fair. Her family was obviously screwed up in their own way, if not quite on the grand scale of his own.

Unless her stepfather or brother turned out to be a killer, of course.

Behind him, she suddenly stumbled and grabbed at his shoulders to avoid going down painfully onto her knees.

Alan reached back for her hand, steadied her and said, "Break time."

"It hasn't been that long since we, um, had sandwiches."

Kissed, too. And she'd listened to his confidences.

He looked to one side so his headlamp didn't blind her. "We should be stopping at least hourly." Which was true. "This is as good a place as any."

Better than most, he realized, seeing the slope of water-washed stone to one side. The picture that flickered in his mind of stripping her after all and laying her back on that nice, smooth surface stirred the beginnings of arousal. Trying to squelch the whole idea, he decided it would be too gritty. And what made him think she would even consider taking a break for wild sex in the middle of this really fun outing?

Glad she couldn't see him very well, he lowered his pack and eased hers off before they both sat down and stretched out their legs.

"I have some candy bars," she offered.

"Sounds better than my energy bars."

"I've been eating way too much candy this summer." That had to be a smile in her voice. She couldn't be too mad at him. "We sell them in the gift shop. There's this big rack, right by the cash register…"

"That you operate."

"Yes!"

Alan chuckled.

She gave him an Almond Joy, a favorite from when he was a kid. He tore open the wrapping and devoured it, hearing her doing the same—although he bet she ate hers more daintily than his three giant bites.

Something he'd been thinking about as they walked, part of his effort to distract himself from that kiss, and he decided to ask. She'd been curious about his past, so how could she be offended if he was equally nosy?

"You don't talk about your mother," he said.

Jo went still. No more rustling of a wrapper, no chewing. Had she quit breathing?

"She left us," she finally said in a small, dry voice.

He frowned. "How old were you?"

"Thirteen."

Her tone was tighter than any choke in this cave. Did those few, spare words rub her throat raw?

"Your brother and sister couldn't have been very old."

"No. Brody was six, Lucy only two. It was…really awful."

He didn't get it. Why had the kids stayed with the father who sounded like something of a jackass? What mother walked out on a toddler?

"Were they fighting?"

This sigh, he heard.

"Yes. Rod is…really controlling. And a sexist jerk, too. One time when he was going off on how women just didn't have the right stuff, I tried to protest." She went quiet for a moment. "It was only a year or two after the divorce. He said, 'Look at your mother. Can't think of a better example. Going got rough, she took off.'"

Alan swore. "What a—" He reined in the word that had come to mind and substituted, "creep."

"*I* thought so."

"Did they fight over custody?"

The air shifted, making Alan realized she'd shaken her head.

"No. She just…took off."

"She didn't talk to you first?"

Another faint stir. "She left a note. Promised to be in touch, but all that came were a scattering of Christmas and birthday cards, and only for a few years. Those years were really hard. I had to try to be a mom to Lucy especially, but Brody, too, and go to school. I hated what she did to us."

"That was a lot for a girl that age to shoulder." His hand found hers, too chilled.

"I tried so hard. I did my best. Only then I abandoned Lucy and Brody when I left for college. I've always felt guilty, but I was desperate. I thought they understood, but Lucy threw that at me when I first came home this summer. She felt deserted, and I don't blame her. For her, it was twice over."

Pity squeezed his heart. "You know that's wrong, don't you? *You* were a kid. Where was Rod?"

"Running the business." She paused. "That's not fair. He had to step up, too. Pay for child care during the hours I was in school, do the driving and grocery shopping. You know. Everything I couldn't take over."

Alan wanted to say something really foul. It was all he could do to refrain. Jo's stepfather had expected a devastated thirteen-year-old girl to become a fill-in mother-housekeeper to keep the household running so his life wasn't impacted any more than necessary? Maybe he was misreading this, but he didn't think so.

He was also hit with the crashing understanding that Jo was a thousand miles away from being the sunny, uncomplicated woman he'd tried to convince himself she was, even though he'd seen the shadows in her eyes from the beginning. She bore as many scars as he did, just a different kind.

Then he got struck by a sickening thought. Keep it to himself? No.

"Sounds like your mother could be said to have disappeared, too."

The words just hung there.

Jo made a ragged sound before she whispered, "Oh, dear God. I never thought—"

He had to put an arm around her. She stayed stiff, quivering with shock, doubt, pain.

"She did send cards." Not hard to guess she hadn't been comforted by those cards. Or even convinced by them? Had she thought Rod might be responsible for them, trying to make his kids feel better?

"You recognized her handwriting?" Alan asked.

"Oh, dear God," Jo said again. "I never understood. Her going that way."

"You didn't believe, deep down, your mom would do anything like that."

"No. We were close! She loved us all. I knew she was unhappy with Rod. I came in on her once crying right after she found out she was pregnant with Lucy. I think maybe she'd been considering leaving Rod, but after that she felt trapped. Two children and pregnant? What could she do for a living?"

"I suppose he had her working in the cavern."

"When she wasn't keeping house and taking care of us kids. She did some of the bookkeeping, too. Of course, he wouldn't have paid her. Unless she stripped joint bank accounts, where would she have gotten money to run?"

Alan wrapped an arm around her. She turned into him and took a handful of his coverall, her hand shaking.

"You didn't say about the handwriting."

"I don't know. I only saw the note she left once. The writing was…ragged, but I thought that meant she was emotional." A swallow. "I was so sure she'd come back for us. I waited and waited. I told myself how lucky I was that Rod never said a word about me not being his child."

Angry, Alan was blunter than he had to be. "Why would he, when you were so useful?"

But she only said, "You're right. I've felt so guilty for letting Brody and Lucy and Rod down later, and now—"

"We don't know," he reminded her. "We may be building…" Not castles in the sky.

Her laugh hurt to hear. "Crypts under the Summerlin Cavern?"

Jo COULDN'T BELIEVE she hadn't ever wondered.

She'd *known*, soul deep, that Mom wouldn't do that to her or Brody and Lucy. And yet she'd bought Rod's story.

If it was a story. How well could a thirteen-year-old girl claim to really know any adult, especially a parent? Kids wanted to believe in their parents. They clung to that faith with fingernails that could penetrate granite.

"Mom wasn't anything like the girls that have disappeared," she argued after a minute. "If that's what you're thinking."

"No, she wasn't." Alan sounded kind, even tender. He must know how hard he'd slammed her. "Maybe the two things don't have anything to do with each other. But you've described a man to me who is controlling to the nth degree and has some contempt for women. He's possessive. Mostly of his land and his cavern, but would he be willing to let his wife go if she took his children with her?"

Really shaking now, Jo held on to a man whose solidity she trusted. "He...he might have offered to let her go, or even Lucy, but never Brody."

"But how could she leave children that young with him?"

Jo was both in shock, and stunned at how thoroughly she'd practiced denial. How could she not have seen this possibility? "If she told him she wanted a divorce, he'd have been enraged."

"I'm sorry," he murmured, his mouth close enough to her ear to ruffle her hair. "Maybe this was a bad time to say anything."

"Because that skull—" Jo couldn't finish. She just couldn't. But a part of her mind was working coldly, clearly. "Even if he did kill Mom, that's not to say he has anything to do with all the women who have gone missing. Only...what if he discovered he enjoyed having ultimate control? Denying her any freedom at all?" Seeing her terror and despair. "Hurting her?"

And wasn't that the worst euphemism ever.

"So eventually he had to replicate the experience," Alan said softly.

She nodded and pressed her face against his chest, wanting a closeness that their multiple layers of clothes denied her. *I don't want to be alone*, she thought with shattering clarity. She always had been, until her eyes had met Alan Burke's. Until they'd exchanged messages she couldn't even decipher.

"I'll feel like a horrible human being if we find out we're wrong," she mumbled.

His chest vibrated with a choked-off laugh.

"I'm so sorry," he said again.

"About?" She raised her head. "Tearing off my blinders?"

"No. About being blind where you were concerned. I tried to convince myself you were a clueless young woman who teaches little kids and doesn't see the real world around her. I'm…scarred, inside and out, and I couldn't see us connecting."

Was he saying…? Despite the anger she felt at her own self-deception and the grief that speared her heart, Jo felt a powerful surge of hope.

"You were here when I needed you," she said. "And, honestly, why would you notice all this stuff I've been hiding even from myself? I tried to tell myself it wasn't healthy to give in to so much anger or the guilt because I didn't totally sacrifice myself for my little brother and sister. I thought maybe if I pretended long enough, pretense would become reality."

"You didn't talk to friends?"

"My friends…aren't that close. They're too nice to understand."

"You might be wrong about that," he said, gentle again.

"Maybe they're all pretending, too." Jo closed her eyes, not that she could see much anyway with only one backup lamp on, and savored the strength she sensed Alan was doing his best to share with her. Then she carefully started to separate herself.

"I'll bet you're also sorry you set yourself up for me to weep all over you." Good try at lightness, she congratulated herself.

"Don't do that," he said. "Did you not hear what I was telling you?"

"I...no." Which wasn't totally honest, but—

"Jo... C'mere." Displaying physical power she'd only suspected, Alan snatched her up and set her across his lap. Then he bent his head and claimed her mouth in a kiss that felt starved, angry, desperate. A kiss that was exactly what she needed.

She flung her arms around his neck and kissed him back with such fervor, he had to step up a gear to match all the emotions and hunger she was throwing at him.

Once he said something like, "I swore I wasn't going to do this," but she paid no attention to it because he'd somehow stripped off her oversuit and the fleece quarter zip she'd worn beneath it and gotten his hand inside her T-shirt. He found his way inside her stretchy sports bra, too, and she arched convulsively at the feel of that big, hot hand engulfing her breast.

She struggled way less effectively to fight her way through his layers of clothing. Not once did she think, *Is this something we should be doing right now?* She *needed* him, couldn't conceive of not becoming one with this man in every possible way. This wasn't simple attraction, maybe never had been, but right now her emotions were a fierce storm.

"Let me," he growled, picked her up again and set her down so he could stand and strip off clothes. The shadow he cast on a wall showed wild hair, disheveled from removing his helmet, a harshly hewn face, broad powerful shoulders.

He spread something behind her—the sleeping bag,

she realized, in a distant part of her mind. And now he was struggling with the laces on one of her boots even as his mouth traveled up her bare belly, his whiskers scraping as he went. The boot dropped off, and he peeled down her pants and long underwear, Jo helping, or maybe impeding, she had no idea. He seemed to lose interest once he had one leg free. His mouth had found her breast and he sucked hard over the stretchy cotton of the bra even as his fingers slid between her thighs. Jo wasn't nearly as good at doing two things at once, but she'd found the zipper that kept her from getting her hand inside his jeans.

It didn't want to cooperate, though, not given the solid ridge beneath. She persevered in the brief intervals when she could concentrate at all, but finally he growled something and took over for that, too. Jo immediately wrapped her hand around him, made even more desperate by the sheer size and power of this man.

"Are you on birth control?"

She bit the hard muscle in his upper arm, all she could reach at that moment.

He was groping in his pack.

Jo's flesh chilled while she waited.

"Man, I'm glad I threw these in," he muttered. He tore the packet and donned the condom.

And then he was kissing her again, his fingers deftly working magic, and she spread her legs even as she tried to pull him closer.

"I want you so damn much," he said roughly, just as he pushed himself slowly inside her.

"Don't stop," she whispered.

He pulled out, drove hard and fast, so deep, she'd never experienced anything like this. All she could do was react: grab him, try to take him even deeper, if that was possible. And she was talking, too, without the slightest idea what she was saying. Pleading, crying out, making incoherent sounds.

She came around him so powerfully, she didn't give him any choice but to join her. The sound wrenched from his chest could have been from the movement of two slabs of rock breaking, being reshaped by an earthquake. Shaken by pleasure that had been both explosive and glorious beyond anything she'd ever known, Jo knew *she'd* been reshaped.

She was terribly afraid she was in love with this complex, damaged, courageous man who might not feel anything even remotely similar for her.

Chapter Thirteen

Grateful they didn't have much chance to talk beyond the practicalities—"Watch your head"—Alan continued to lead the way. It began to eat at him that he'd said so little, but in truth he wasn't sure what would have been kind to her and right for him. He had to do some thinking.

Now wasn't the time for that. He couldn't afford another serious distraction. As it was, he found himself glad several times when passages split to recognize human-made scratches on the limestone walls. They were distinctive enough, he recognized his own style. Only twice did he see ones he thought Drew might have been responsible for. Alan suspected he'd been determined even then to take care of essentials himself. Lucky those scratches had survived. He'd have found the way without help from the kid he'd been, but it would have taken longer, and his sense of urgency kept mounting.

He guessed from Jo's silence and determination that she felt something similar. Either that, or she was able to block out weariness by brooding about a past that

might not have been anything like she'd wanted to believe it was. Alan half hoped they'd learn that he'd been
wrong—but once he'd suggested her mother was the
first woman to disappear, the pieces of the entire puz-
zle had dropped too damn neatly into place.

Because of that, he had begun to feel some deep fore-
boding. He should be here with real backup, not a vulnerable woman who was confident in this environment,
sure, but didn't carry a gun and wouldn't know how to
respond to violence.

In theory, with his experience he could handle Rod
Summerlin, but Rod had the advantage of knowing this
part of the cavern far better than Alan did. If Alan went
down, could Jo find her way out of here? Could she
move fast enough if her stepfather was on her heels?

Alan gritted his teeth. Would she be willing to stay
behind and wait for him? He knew that answer.

Knee-deep in a stream, recognizing the low-slung
ceiling ahead, he paused.

"You okay?" he asked quietly.

"Fine."

How many times had she said that?

"We're getting close." He kept his voice low. "I don't
hear anything, but we're no more than a quarter of a
mile from the party hall you described."

"Oh. I told you I went a little way past that, but—"

Not far enough, he suspected. And maybe that was
just as well, since she'd been alone that day. She hadn't
said where her stepfather had been when she sneaked
in here. If she'd dawdled and he'd gone looking for her,
Alan had a bad feeling she would have disappeared, too.

"Once we're out of the stream, we'll have to crawl for a short stretch ahead," he told her. "After that, our voices will carry, so let's keep it down."

Her head bobbed. The strain showed on her face in this eerie mix of shadow and light playing off the walls and odd planes that formed the ceiling, but anger and that determination were there, too. She didn't ask if he thought they'd find anything. She had to know they might not, but they'd keep looking as long as it took, Alan vowed. As long as they could do so uninterrupted, he amended. They didn't have to make it all the way back out to his property; they could spend the night whenever he sensed her energy flagged. He still had nuts and energy bars in his pack.

He also carried a Glock handgun in a side pocket of his pack. Next stop, he'd pull it out and tuck it where it would be more accessible.

He tried not to splash any more than necessary, and realized when he stepped out of the water that Jo had fallen behind, partly because she, too, was trying to move quietly. He waited and gave her a hand scrambling out.

"Where's your stepfather this time of day?"

She blinked a few times. "Uh… It's still morning, isn't it?"

He pulled back his glove to reveal a standard wristwatch. "Almost eleven."

"He should be at work. Either leading tours, helping in the gift shop or manning the cash register. Even if he found someone to replace me for the day, he never slows down."

"Good."

"He go out at night?"

She nodded. "Mostly, he takes his truck. I thought he might have a girlfriend. Sometimes he walks back to the gift shop where his office is."

In other words, the SOB had plenty of leisure time in the evenings to pursue his victims.

Unclenching his jaw, Alan said, "Okay. This should be ideal timing for us to poke around then. This might be a good place for us to leave our packs. We don't want to be slowed down."

He could come back if they needed the first aid supplies, but silence and speed had to come first right now.

Jo nodded and set hers down. He did the same, but took out the handgun and slipped it in a pocket of his cargo pants. He looked up to see her gaping at him.

"You came…armed?" she whispered.

"We wouldn't be here if I hadn't tried to prepare for anything."

She chewed on her lower lip and finally nodded.

"If we happen on something unexpected, you go back. Don't try to be heroic. Stay unseen if you can. You got me?"

That might be a glare, but he didn't give a damn. If they were to find anything unpleasant, he wanted to see it first. And if Rod Summerlin just happened to be back here during a break from his tours—say, he'd claimed to be taking lunch—Alan didn't want him setting eyes on Jo.

He thought for a minute she'd argue, but she clamped her mouth shut and waited while he lowered himself to his knees and forearms, both of which were padded. His mouth twitched at the memory of having to hunt down one of her pads, which he'd apparently tossed quite a way while disrobing her.

Despite the fact that he was pushing himself forward with his face inches from the rocky floor of the compressed passage, his body reacted to the memory. Their kisses hadn't been the only revelation; making love with this woman had seriously rattled him. Maybe knowing what to say wouldn't be as hard as he'd thought. Nonetheless, that conversation wasn't happening until they'd seen whatever there was to see and were well on their way out of this damn cavern.

Momentarily stuck, he grunted, released a breath and lowered his hips, going for a snakelike propulsion.

Not much bothered by claustrophobia, he was still glad when space opened in front of him, the beam of his headlamp finding a small room rimmed with young stalactites and stalagmites. As he watched, a drop fell from the closest stalactite. Geology in action. A memory surfaced: the word *stalactite* came from the Greek *stalasso*, or "to drip."

He rose to his feet and helped Jo to rise, too. A sound came to him, distant and too soft to identify, rising and falling, rising and falling. Damn it, was he imagining the occasional hitch?

"Do you hear—?" Jo whispered.

"Yeah," he murmured into her ear, so close his lips brushed her.

"I think… I think that's what I heard that day."

He could see why she'd assumed it was one of the

natural sounds of the cavern, water or wind entering a crack. Or even that she was imagining it altogether; spend long enough in a cave, and you started hearing things that weren't there. Especially if you were unnerved to start with.

But they hadn't dreamed this up since they were hearing the same thing.

"This room would be a good place to hide things," he said, still making sure his voice wouldn't carry. "Did you get this far?"

Jo shook her head. "One of the passages I looked at was blocked by a cave-in and one just seemed to go on and on. The last one was narrow but not that bad. I just got nervous about how much time had passed."

"Okay. Let's look around before we go on."

They split up, Alan feeling comfortable because she wouldn't be far from him at any point. He'd hear anyone else approaching; few people had the training he did to move like a ghost. Once he knew she was turned away, he unsealed the Velcro securing the pocket holding his gun.

The darkness in the crack he investigated first suggested that it opened into one of the dizzying number of alternative passages. He stood sideways, thrusting his arm as far as he could reach, letting the flashlight illuminate a short distance. Beyond was nothing but more darkness. And, although sound could be hard to trace in the labyrinth down here, he felt confident the faint noise wasn't coming from this fissure.

Anyway, he'd seen a photo of a self-satisfied Rod

Summerlin on the cavern website, something he'd looked up only after meeting Jo the day of the search.

Summerlin wouldn't be squeezing through here, Alan felt confident. The guy wasn't heavy—or at least he hadn't been when the photo was taken—but his stocky build wasn't ideal for cave exploration.

For that matter, Alan thought wryly, neither was his, not once he'd added serious muscle to a boy's rangy body.

He backed out and immediately turned to see what Jo was doing.

The beam of light settled on her shapely butt as she bent over to peer into an odd-shaped opening. Satisfied for the moment, he swept his light around the perimeter of the room, looking for anything of interest. Nothing in particular caught his eye, but he moved toward the deep shadows behind an enormous boulder.

A strangled choking sound had him spinning around.

Jo had backed out by the time he crouched beside her.

"Dear God," she whispered hoarsely. She seemed unable to tear her eyes from the darkness beyond her headlamp beam.

Alan grasped her shoulders and turned her. "What?"

Her throat worked, her gaze now fastened desperately on him. "Bones," she finally managed.

"A skeleton?"

Her teeth chattered. "More than one."

"Damn it." He tugged her closer and wrapped her in a tight embrace. She burrowed in and shook. The tough woman he'd gotten to know, the one determined to face the nightmare from her past, wouldn't let herself cry.

Then he eased her back and said, "Let me look."

He had to crouch but not crawl. Three feet in, his beam found a chamber that might be five by ten feet. And no, she hadn't imagined anything; there was indeed a jumble of bones.

To one side a skull gave the chilling impression that it was staring at him. Damn, there was a second skull. Neither were near the opening, and he didn't see any scratches on either to suggest a dog's teeth had closed on it. So…there might well be a third, somewhere.

Studying the scattered and heaped bones, he shook his head on that thought. What he saw had to come from five or six bodies, at a minimum. His guess that this serial killer had found victims they didn't yet know about was accurate.

Fabric, or the remnants of garments, was tangled with the bones. Bodies had been heaved in here, next to or atop one another. No care taken, probably no posing. Unlike some serial killers, this guy hadn't been interested in the women once they were dead, except to be sure their remains weren't found. The resulting jumble had occurred because of decomposition and the effects of gravity.

Amy Kendall, he couldn't help thinking, wasn't here. She'd disappeared too recently to be down to bones yet.

Alan continued to sweep the small room with his beam. The ceiling was wet, dripping, the walls slick, almost slimy looking. Water seemed to be draining into a crack or hole toward the far-right corner.

Sickened although he'd seen worse in war zones, Alan rolled his shoulders to release tension. With some effort, he located his phone. Resting on his elbows, he tapped on the photo function and began taking pictures. A couple of dozen, recording as completely as he could the hideous gravesite just in case Rod Summerlin had enough warning to clear it out. As an afterthought, he pulled out the Swiss Army knife he carried in a pocket, looked for an obscure place and scratched both his initials and the date low on the wall.

Then Alan backed out. "I'm sorry," he said simply to Jo, whose shock had turned into something worse. She had that thousand-yard stare he recognized.

"I saw some fabric," she whispered. "Pink with flowers."

Oh, damn; he'd seen that. It had to be synthetic to have survived virtually intact.

"My mother wore that blouse all the time."

NO SUSPICIONS HAD prepared her for anything like this. On some level, she'd wanted to think she was suffering from paranoia, that Rod was the man she'd always believed him to be.

Now she knew. Who else would have killed her mother just as she'd asked for a divorce? *My mother's bones are right there, a few feet away. They've been there all these years, so near. That might be her skull with the dark, accusing eye sockets.*

Jo wished she could believe that the darkness where eyes should have been made Rod even the least bit squeamish. But of course not—if he possessed a grain of conscience, he'd have smashed the skull in rage.

Hard reality hit Jo.

Mom hadn't written that note, or any of the later ones. Only Rod could have done that. Likely Mom would have offered to find a job in Mayville, stay close enough for Rod to see his kids often, but that hadn't been good enough. He'd have been humiliated with townspeople knowing his wife had left him. Letting her, Brody, Lucy and even, maybe, Jo slip out of his control had been more than he could countenance.

Jo wondered dully if he'd struck out without intending to kill her mother, if Mom had fallen and hit her head or something like that. Although, neither of the skulls she'd been able to see had a noticeable indentation.

Had Rod shocked himself by his willingness to kill? He'd been strange in the weeks after she'd thought her mother had left, Jo remembered. Then, that had seemed natural. Of course, he was hurt, his whole life turned on end.

You mean, he flipped all their lives on end, she thought grimly.

I hate him.

But what if she was wrong, and someone else had killed Mom? There could have been an employee back then who who'd started his killing spree with Mom, who was readily available, and kept a key all these years to be sure of continuing access to the cavern. There could be someone else—say, Austin, who'd found Mom's bones and been inspired to do something awful he'd only toyed with before. Or to start stashing victims in the caves instead of whatever he'd done with them before.

She *wanted* to believe Rod didn't have anything to do with this, but she wouldn't kid herself, either. Too much pointed to Rod. He'd had reason to kill his wife, to deceive the children into believing she had deserted them. He had the best access to the cavern, had been furious at the very idea of any of them venturing past the show portion of the cavern. And then there was his thinly veiled disdain for women.

"I wish I'd thought to bring bolt cutters," Alan muttered, pulling her back to the moment. "We could walk right out there, to hell with the tours, and have the police here in minutes."

"But you didn't believe me."

"Did you believe yourself?"

Feeling so much she was, paradoxically, almost numb, she said, "No. Now… That sounds an awful lot like a woman is crying."

Fierce eyes met hers. "Yeah. It does."

Jo felt sick. If only she'd gone farther that day, the crying woman wouldn't have suffered for so much longer. "We have to go on."

"I'd be happier if you'd wait here."

Somehow, she'd known he would say that, and had already made up her mind.

"I dragged you here. Not the other way around. I'm not stopping."

She suspected his mumble was profane, but ignored it.
"Okay." He rose to his feet. "You'll stay behind me."

She could do that. If ever she'd met a man able to
meet violence with violence, it was Alan Burke, former navy SEAL and police detective. She was fiercely
glad of that. After his honesty about his past, after their
lovemaking, she knew she could trust him as she never
had anyone else since her mother.

"Quiet from here on out." He softened the order by
taking her hand in his and squeezing with remarkable
gentleness.

Jo only wished their hands had been bare. She tried
to smile but knew her attempt for an abysmal failure.
He must have recognized that she'd tried, though, because he dipped his head and kissed her, quick but expressing an astonishing amount.

Then he led the way toward the passage from which
she, too, thought the ghostly crying came.

Jo was glad she no longer carried her pack. Lighter
on her feet, she'd be able to move with more stealth.
She hoped.

The ceiling sloped down, but not as low as in the
previous passage, thank goodness.

Alan kept his headlamp on, but she left hers off. Her
hands brushed the soles of his boots, and she kept her
eyes on the dark silhouette of him against the glow.
Her breath came faster as the crying gained in volume. No, it still could be a natural phenomenon, she
wanted to believe. Surely, *surely*, Rod wouldn't im-
prison a woman for any length of time so close to the
show portions of the cavern.

Except, it was far enough, at most even those in the party room had heard a suggestion of sound. If poor Jesse hadn't been lured by the dog, Jo and Alan wouldn't be here now. They wouldn't have found the grave site that gave answers to the grieving parents of all these young women.

A part of her mind still had trouble accepting what she'd seen. She'd grown up here, had led countless tours proceeding only a short distance away. Never *imagined*—

And why would she? Most of the time, Rod seemed like an okay guy. Hadn't he been genuinely worried about Lucy?

Or was it that he wanted Jo to shut her up?

She'd quit concentrating on stealth. Her knee whacked a rock that rolled, making noise.

Please not a skull, she thought, in the absolute silence that followed. Alan had frozen; the crying had halted.

"Is someone there?" a young female voice called. It was thin, scared, pleading. "Help! Please!"

Jo wanted desperately to answer, but hesitated. Thank God, because the next thing she heard was a roar of rage and the careless scraping of feet rushing toward them, a nimbus of light dancing over the uneven walls.

Alan began to back up, forcing her to do the same, as hard as it was to hurry when scrabbling backward. She hurt by the time she reached the larger room and leaped up.

"Quickly," Alan growled.

Her mouth opened to protest, but instead she obeyed, dropping into the next crawl.

Gunfire erupted behind her, terrifyingly loud.

Alan grunted and fell forward as something solid clattered on rock. He hadn't been the one firing his gun, she knew in horror. He'd been shot!

Chapter Fourteen

Once an operation stumbled into chaos, there was no resetting the clock.

Alan knew he couldn't rely on his right arm, and the Glock had dropped from his hand.

Rolling, groping for his gun with his left hand, he kept thinking with cold clarity. It was worth trying to convince Rod this had all been a big misunderstanding.

Unless and until he could line up a shot of his own.

"What the *hell*?" he yelled. Fortunately, he'd never spoken before to this man, who wouldn't recognize his voice. "We're cavers! We're not doing anything!"

Another shot rang out and chips of limestone flew.

If only he and Jo had gotten to the girl—or were there two of them?—a minute sooner, he'd have been prepared had anyone arrived to check on his victim. As it was, Alan didn't have to turn on a light to know his shirt and coverall were soaked with blood and if he stood up, his arm would dangle uselessly at his side. He was a decent shot with his left hand, but not as good as with his right. If he took the offensive and failed, Jo would be left vulnerable—and in the past few hours, *she* had become his priority.

"Go," he growled at her. "We have to hide."

What they had to do was get out of the caves to find help, and do it fast enough to keep the madman behind them from killing again and then cleaning house. Even if Alan had believed he and Jo could retreat the way they'd come, the trip would take too long.

Time for Plan B.

She grabbed his hand. "You're bloody!"

Quiet anguish. All he could say was, "Shot. Let's move."

He had to shove his gun into a pocket to free his good hand to grab the pack. What did he do then in this damn darkness but stumble over hers?

No time to stop. He doubted she had anything essential in it. He pushed her ahead of him, glad she seemed to know where she was going. Drop low, crawl, squirm through the tightest stretch while dragging his pack. His right shoulder hurt like a— He didn't even let himself think the rest. No time to dwell. He'd been injured before and continued to function.

A hint of light glowed behind them. The gunman wasn't going to let them go. Either he was insane, or he had somehow guessed these intruders weren't innocent adventurers.

With a resounding *crack*, another shot skimmed the side of the passage. A chip of rock stung Alan's cheek. Jo made a whimpering sound but never stopped, scrambling as fast as he would have been able to go, anyway.

A scrape, a gasp and a splash of water came from ahead. Jo had emerged and tumbled into the stream.

"Left," he gasped. He'd never hoped more that his memory was solid.

"But we came—"

"Do what I say." Under fire his men followed his orders without argument. Until the one time they didn't. Apologize to Jo later.

Without light, he ended up on his hand and knees in the water. Trying to get to his feet, he almost lost the pack. *Can't afford to*, he told himself coldly. Not given where they were going.

Jo wasn't moving very fast anymore. How could she with no light? His recollection of this route was too vague for them to stumble entirely in the dark. The danger of them blundering into a deadly hazard was greater than that of them getting shot.

"Turn your light on," he said, voice scraping in his throat. "Get a quick look ahead."

She did. He blinked, needing his eyes to readjust. "Out of the water."

Another shot, this one going God knew where, but it served as a warning. Jo plunged them back into darkness without waiting for his command. She kept going, too, although he could hear the whistle of her breathing. Not lack of conditioning, he thought, but rather fear.

"We're going, we're going!" Alan yelled, straining to hear any sounds from behind him.

As they fled, he debated finding a hiding place to set up an ambush. That would have been his first choice, except for two factors: his injury, and the reality that

the man chasing them knew these caves better than
Alan or Jo did. He'd have explored in every direction
before settling on the dumping ground for bodies and
the best place to hold his captives. The question was,
would he believe that the intruders weren't anybody
he needed to worry about, or would he continue to
pursue them?

Or, worse possibility, go back to erase everyone and
everything that could condemn him?

Having no answer, all Alan could do was push Jo on,
ignore the agony in his shoulder and the more frightening numbness in his arm and hand, and keep going.
They had to get far enough ahead of this crazy SOB
to be able to set up a descent into another level of the
cavern.

Yeah, and hope Jo wouldn't balk at sliding down a
rope into impenetrable darkness.

ALL JO COULD DO was grope her way forward in a passage too wide for her to touch each side at the same
time. She wished Alan was leading, but knew why he
hung back.

How badly was he hurt? That grunt had told her he
was injured even before he said, *Shot*. If he'd dropped
his gun, had he been able to find it? She'd give a lot to
be able to *see* him, if only for a moment, to evaluate
his condition with her own eyes.

Her flattened hand her only guide, she took care with
every step. She could so easily walk right into a sta-
lagmite rising from the floor or fall over a loose rock
or intrusion. If she were injured enough to slow them

down even more, Rod would kill them. Jo had no doubt about it.

She didn't let herself question where Alan was taking them. Even more, she couldn't think about that terrified voice.

Is someone there? Help! A whimpered, *Please?*

No! She'd become paralyzed if she let herself focus on anything but fleeing.

The rough wall suddenly wasn't there. Jo stopped, then, without consulting Alan, switched on her headlamp. The passage curved, that's all, and angled downward. Water entered from a crevice up above and ran down the sides, making the cave floor ahead glisten.

Turning off the light, she told herself, *Careful, careful*, and hurried forward.

Twice she slipped, once staggering into the wet wall where she was able to right herself. The second time, she thought she was going down on her butt, but a strong arm caught her and set her back on her feet.

"Are you all right?" she whispered.

"Fine. Keep going."

O-kay.

Once she turned her head and thought she saw a very faint glow behind them, enough for Alan to rear as a tall, dark silhouette. She prayed she was imagining it just because she knew he was there, that there really *wasn't* any light.

The air felt close, her every step louder than it should have been. Alan...no, she could hear him, too, and the incessant trickle of water. This flight couldn't have lasted more than minutes—ten? fifteen?—but felt in-

terminable. She had no idea how long they'd been underway. Was Rod really chasing them?

How could he let them go? she thought hopelessly.
Even if they were some weekend cavers who'd stum-
bled into the Summerlin Cavern, if they found their
way out, they'd report someone shooting at them.
Wouldn't they? That would bring the police to Rod.
He didn't dare risk any interest from law enforcement.

Her thighs burned. She wasn't sure she could feel
the fingers she grazed on the wall, although how could
they be cold when she wore gloves?

Behind, Alan said suddenly, "Grab onto me anywhere
you can. I need to go ahead. We should be coming on
a shaft."

A shaft? As in, a *hole*? Did it go up, or— No, of course
not. They wouldn't be able to climb. So where did it descend *to*? Did he know? And even if he and his friend
had explored this far when they were boys, how could
Alan trust in the accuracy of his memories?

Not like this was any moment to question him. Stepping to one side, she let him by and grabbed for the pack
he'd slung over his left shoulder. Her fingers closed on
the coil of rope strapped to the outside.

He was already moving, and she had to jog a couple
of steps to keep up.

This was why he carried the rope, she realized queasily. Not expecting to need it but prepared for anything.
She'd vaguely known the cavern was multilevel. It almost had to be, right? The tour entrance gaped about
halfway up the ridge. She'd always known water trickled downward from above. That's how these caves were

formed. And no, water didn't just trickle; depending on the season, it tumbled. And where had she thought all that water was going? Some of it might escape to cascade down the steep exposed hillside into the river, but it made more sense that there was at least one level below the cavern she'd thought she knew, possibly more.

Had the sinkhole once been part of this cave complex?

She stumbled and wrenched her mind back to what she was doing. Every footstep, every uneasy glance over her shoulder. No hint of light. If Rod was back there, he couldn't move any faster than they were able to in the dark, because even a small flashlight would pinpoint his location. He might risk that if he didn't suspect these two people—or did he think there was only one?—had been investigating the sound of crying and the skull a boy had claimed to see.

A splashing sound beneath her feet pulled her back to the here and now. She was having more and more trouble holding onto clarity. Water wasn't just slick now, it had to be an inch or two deep. In winter and early spring, this stream would probably be a flood, possibly impassable. Given the complete darkness and only a sense of resistance against her feet, she couldn't tell for sure how deep the water had become now, and did it matter anyway? Except, the sound of splashing might keep her from hearing someone drawing closer to them from behind.

Alan paused and turned on his headlamp. She had to squeeze her eyes shut against the shocking brightness.

He muttered to himself and changed course. The light vanished. She stumbled after him, blinking against the after-flash.

HE CAME ON the pit so suddenly he was damn lucky not to walk right off the edge of it. Alan doubted Jo's grip was strong enough to pull him back if he'd teetered.

While he shut down that surge of adrenalin, he had no choice but to turn his light on again and search the rough edges of the giant hole for a formation of rock strong enough and shaped right to sling the rope around. He hated what he was going to force Jo to do, the risks he was taking for both of them, but this still seemed to be the best option. He and Drew had done this, albeit long ago. The drop hadn't been so great as to leave them dangling with no choice but to somehow climb back up or release the rope and fall an unknown distance.

Pain wasn't helping the clarity of his memories, though. Was this the place he thought it was?

Tuck Jo somewhere safe, lie in wait for her stepfather. Maybe that would still be the better option.

His gut said no. They needed backup.

The beam of his light stopped on the broken bottom of a column that made him think of a giant tooth. Moving as fast as he could, he uncoiled the rope, turned on his headlamp and struggled to form an Italian hitch. With his right hand refusing to cooperate, he had to ask Jo for help. Either she knew her knots, or she understood what he was trying to do, and if her fingers moved slower than he liked, they got it done. He clipped on a carabiner, and then straightened. When he dropped his pack over the edge, Jo cried out, but he said, "There's nothing breakable in it." Then he said, "You have to go now."

She whispered, "I didn't hear the pack hit bottom."

"We don't have any choice, Jo. I've descended this shaft before. You won't kill yourself letting go when you get to the end of the rope."

He saw her terror and gave her a single, hard kiss. "Turn on your lamp as soon as you're over the lip."

She'd had enough training to know how to wrap the ropes around her body to allow her to rappel. All he could see was her face, the fear and yet the resolution. If she'd been frozen with terror…hell. They'd have been screwed.

He had her turn off his headlamp before she went, and she had the guts to back off the edge into the dark abyss with no benefit of light.

Any caver knew that what they were doing was by default foolish, maybe even suicidal. Normally, he'd have set up anchors, have carried more ropes. What he'd fashioned—all he'd had time for—was called a pull-through. The descent could be made by abseil, and at the bottom the caver could retrieve his rope by pulling. Simple—but what this kind of descent didn't allow was retreat. There was no way back up. The caver could only go on. In this case, "on" wasn't a complete mystery, but it was damned hazy in his memory.

He followed her descent by the circle of light that accompanied her. When she called up, "I'm at the end," he could tell from her voice that she couldn't see the bottom of this hole.

When she said, "I'm letting go," he closed his eyes and prayed like he hadn't ever in his life.

A thud was followed by an involuntarily cry. And then a shaken voice saying, "I'm okay. Hurry."

Thank God.

He followed, bracing his feet against the rough wall of the shaft, and let the rope slide between his gloved hands—yeah, he'd managed to bend his elbow and manually place the fingers of his right hand where they needed to be, whether they'd be any use or not—and tighten painfully on his thigh.

He let himself drop with foolish haste into the dark abyss.

To be out of the way, Jo retreated a few feet into what appeared to be a passage and waited. They'd be okay once he got down here, wouldn't they? Rod would have no reason to have been carrying rope of his own, and he wouldn't be able to stop Alan from yanking on one end and whipping the rope through the carabiner and loose.

Hugging herself, she tipped her head up to give him some light. She only knew he was on his way down because of the way the pack swung. Alan himself was still in darkness when a light appeared at the top.

She wanted to scream out his name, but he wasn't blind. Rod—if this was Rod—was crouching, she could tell that much. If he started shooting methodically—

The pack and the rope and Alan all plummeted at the same time. Their pursuer had cut the rope, she realized, starting forward. Alan had been too high. How could he survive?

Heavier than the pack, he hit at almost the same moment, the rope whipping to lash him. Belatedly, Jo turned off her lamp. She heard a deep groan, movement—she thought—and then gunfire, so much she clapped her hands over her ears.

The fusillade was followed by silence and darkness.

And she couldn't move, couldn't make a sound, or give away that she, at least, had lived.

She had to have waited two or three minutes when she dared hope the monster had gone away.

Terribly afraid she was whimpering, Jo stumbled forward. "Alan? Alan?"

"Yeah." That was his voice, oh, thank God, but it was a pained rasp.

"Are you…?"

"Don't…know."

Those words hurt to hear.

She turned on her headlamp. She had to *see* him.

He'd either bounced or rolled six or eight feet away from the pack and the pile of rope. Holes pocked the pack. Alan was bleeding, but maybe no more than he already had been? Jo didn't know.

She fell to her knees beside him. "Where are you hurt?"

"We can't stay out here." He sounded stronger. "Let's get out of sight from up above."

"Let me help."

"I'll roll. Grab the pack. We might need it."

She rose to her feet and scurried forward, her skin

crawling at the possibility they were being watched from above. He could have snapped a new magazine in the handgun she hadn't known he owned. But she seized the pack by a strap and a handful of the rope and retreated as fast as she could.

Alan had somehow moved a few yards into the passage and levered himself into a sitting position, back against a rough wall.

When she reached him, he lifted a hand and tried to poke a gloved finger into one of the holes in the pack. "I think it's dead."

"You're joking about it," she said in disbelief.

He grimaced. "Why not?"

She'd been wrong; his face was bloody, but only as if it had been scraped. The helmet had to have protected his head when he hit the rock floor, but she could see that his headlamp was smashed. Jo wanted to laugh. She wanted to cry. What she did was reach out and grab his good hand.

He squeezed hers so hard, it hurt, but she never wanted to let go.

GETTING TO HIS feet was bad enough. Digging deep through the cotton in his head for his memory of that single, long-ago trip through this lower level of the great Summerlin Cavern was harder.

It all got worse when Jo said suddenly, "I think that was Lucy."

He'd decided not to discard anything from his pack. If they got lost, they'd need it all. Then Jo's words sank in. "What?"

"I'm pretty sure that was Lucy calling for help." Jo's misery was clear. "I told you she wasn't in her bed this morning. I think…she was refusing to give up. He was getting madder and madder, and… I think I said before. If she did find the key last night, and Rod caught her in the cavern, how could he let her go?"

Yeah, Alan bet that's what happened. If Lucy had gotten far enough to discover Amy, or even bloody handcuffs… Or, hell, bones."

"Anyway, Brody is important to him. I doubt Lucy ever really was."

"We can't be a hundred percent sure the killer isn't someone else who caught Lucy back here," Alan reminded her. "Rod brought you home—" he broke off.

"I guess he thought I'd reason with her, and all would be well. He could go on his usual way."

She believed it was Rod after them, and Alan thought the same. Realistically, could an armed stranger stroll into the cavern, then back out again, certain he'd been unseen? *This* visit hadn't been in the middle of the night.

Jo wasn't crying, but he heard the equivalent of a deep, painful bruise in her voice. If it turned out they were wrong, Alan could only imagine the relief she'd feel.

"All we can do is hurry," he said, knowing how completely that failed as reassurance, but it was true. They had no time to waste.

After a moment, she asked, "Can you go on?"

"I've functioned when I was in worse shape."

"Is there anything I can do?"

"Maybe take a look at my shoulder. Might be able to wrap it." The sharp stab in his hip, the wrenching pain in his neck that he suspected was the equivalent of whiplash, at least kept him from feeling the more generalized hurt that would undoubtedly manifest in bruises up and down his body.

"I don't know what I was thinking!" She scrambled to her feet. "Oh, God. Your arm is soaked with blood. What if you're—"

"Bleeding out?" he said dryly. "If I were, I'd be dead by now." As she tugged at his oversuit, he cooperated until she had his arm and shoulder freed. Then he stopped her when she reached for the buttons on his flannel shirt. "No, that might not go back on over a heavy bandage. Let's just try to stabilize it and get going."

He'd brought first aid supplies, including heavy gauze pads and vet wrap, which she used to wrap his shoulder with reasonable expertise. Maybe everyone who worked at the cavern took first aid classes. As she sank back on her haunches, she looked doubtful. "I don't know if that will do any good. A sling would be a good idea, but—"

He'd need to use the arm to the extent it was capable. Yeah.

He insisted they take a drink from the one water bottle that hadn't been punctured by bullet holes and to each eat a handful of nuts. Unfortunately, neither gave him a magical boost in energy. He also swallowed several painkillers, but if they were going to help, it would take time.

Then he reached for his pack.

"No!" Jo snatched it from him. "I'll carry it."

He'd like to have argued but couldn't. He coiled the two pieces of rope and used the Velcro tab to hang them from the pack.

He was just forcing himself to his feet when Jo asked straight-out, "Is there a way out? Can you find it?"

Given their extreme stress and danger, a lie might be the best thing he could do for her right now.

Chapter Fifteen

Whether Alan had been completely honest about their chances of making it out—or out in time to have even a remote chance of saving Lucy—Jo had no idea. All she could do was trust him. He'd gotten her this far. Her fear was that they couldn't move fast enough. Why leave Lucy alive?

Alan had claimed there was an opening to this cave less than half an hour away. Unfortunately, it would bring them out on a steep side hill much like the one where the bobcat had startled her. However, he remembered a dirt road directly beneath, one used by fishermen following the river.

"Drew and I had a hell of a hike home," he'd added wryly. "No fisherman around that day."

And he hadn't dared call his own father for a lift, she assumed.

Right now, she was awed at the strength that allowed a man who'd been shot and had lost more blood than she wanted to think about and who'd plummeted so far to a rocky landing that should have killed him to still move fast enough to avoid the bullets that would have finished him off. Somehow, he was already on his feet holding a light in his hand and leading her with rare hesitations through a maze of cave passages that were wetter than those above. She gave a shuddery thought to the increased heaviness of earth above them before dismissing it.

A couple of places where Alan made a choice of which direction to go he stopped for long moments first, rubbing his gloved hand over the shiny wet limestone until he seemingly found…something.

Glancing back at her once, he said, "Drew or I marked turns when we were kids."

Twice, he stopped and said, "This isn't right," and they turned back to the previous intersection.

A few times they crossed large spaces, one a spectacular showroom displaying rippling flowstones like the grandest of stage curtains and enormous columns as awe-inspiring as those supporting Greek temples. Another time, she might have taken pictures, but right now, all she could think about was Lucy. What was happening? How much time had passed?

And then she stopped at a sudden realization. "My phone was in my pack."

Alan swung both the light and his head toward her, momentarily blinding her. "We might be able to find it later."

Later.

"Unless *he* picks up my pack."

"Is there anything in it that would identify you?"

Throat tight, she shook her head. "Except my phone,

but he wouldn't be able to open it. You have yours, don't you?"

"Yeah." He patted a pocket. "Lucky, since I have Drew's number."

Jo nodded and followed him when he started out again.

He must be in agony, unless he'd passed through that to a merciful numbness. Until she had that thought, Jo hadn't acknowledged, or really even noticed, that *she* hurt, too, from the hours and hours they'd hiked through the rough terrain, the stretches of crawling or creeping, the rope descent, the fear.

None of which mattered compared to her fear for her sister.

When he stopped, she walked right into him. They'd come to…a waterfall? No, she saw, a tumultuous stream was a better description. And there didn't seem to be any way to go but into the water.

He turned around. "We're close to the end, Jo, I promise. This is the tough stretch, though. We have to lie on our backs and let the stream take us. We might be completely underwater for fifteen or twenty seconds at a time. Most of the time, there'll be some air at the top of the passage."

Most of the time.

She replayed what he'd said and didn't like it any better this time.

"If you don't think you can do it, you can wait here. I'll come back for you. I'll leave you with lights and my pack. There's food in there, warm clothes—"

Jo shook her head even though she didn't think she'd ever been so scared. "No. I'm not staying behind."

She was enough shorter, her light cast strange shadows on his face again, but she saw intensity and a struggle on his face.

Then he said huskily, "You're an amazing woman."

She tipped forward and wrapped her arms around him. The need for speed kept either from savoring the closeness for any length of time, but it helped.

"I'll have to leave my pack," he said, squatting and setting it down. "Let me find—"

What he had to find, apparently, were waterproof bags. She understood why when he deposited his phone and then his big gun in different ones. As a seeming afterthought, he took off his wristwatch and dropped it in one, too, before stowing both in pockets in his cargo pants.

"Okay," he said, still in that rough voice, "I think you should go first."

Because she was smaller, less likely to get stuck. So she could go on if he couldn't make it, and get help for Lucy.

As fast as the water seemed to be running, would he be able to retreat if he got stuck?

He knows what he's doing, she told herself. This was a different kind of trust. So she only nodded.

NOSE BARELY ABOVE WATER, Alan reached ahead to feel the cave ceiling dropping. Jo had gone through; at least, she wasn't thrashing right ahead, desperate for air.

Alan took a deep breath and propelled himself forward using his feet against the walls of the shrinking passage and his hand on the ceiling.

Maybe he'd tell Deputy Ed Madsen that he'd lost interest in cave diving, he thought with near humor.

The distraction worked long enough for him to find the next pocket of air. *If there was a hell*, he thought, *this might be it.* Or not. He'd seen plenty of forms of hell during operations around the world.

His shoulders wedged him to a stop in an especially narrow spot, although one that, thank God, allowed him to keep his mouth and nose above water. Wriggling to break the logjam wasn't as easy when the one shoulder and arm were laggardly about obeying commands, but he managed and let the water carry him on.

He saw Jo's face again, starkly lit, her determination to do anything to save the sister she loved so clear. If she could love him like that—

It might be too soon to think that way, but Alan knew that if she died in this cave, he wouldn't be getting over these feelings. He'd do anything to kill the bastard that had stolen her mother from her and destroyed and damaged so many other lives.

Another deep breath, another stretch to let the water carry him.

The next time he lifted his mouth for air, he not only found plenty to suck in, he saw that the stream was widening and the ceiling raised. He was seeing because daylight penetrated the cave. At first it was diffuse, almost an illusion, then brighter and brighter. Rolling in the water, knees bumping rocks, he crashed into a larger obstacle, and a hand reached for him.

"What *took* you so long?"

Pushing himself to his knees and taking in Jo's anguished expression, Alan said, "I'm bigger than you. I was more like a cork that kept getting stuck than a piece of sediment that flowed out with the wine."

A sound escaped her that might have been either a laugh or a sob, and she shook her head. "Look! It's beautiful!"

Getting to his feet, he did look, and she was right. Water tumbled over sharp gray rocks in a glittering cascade toward the winding river that cut through the valley below. The typical mix of deciduous trees in the Missouri woods were in bright green leaf. The sky arched above, a pure blue. And there was a dirt track along the river, just as he'd remembered.

Prettiest of all was the soaking wet, battered and exhausted woman beside him.

Alan gave her a jubilant hug, a brief, passionate kiss, then ripped off his glove with his teeth and reached in the pocket with the phone. Jo took the bag from him and opened it. He went to his most recent calls and touched Drew's name.

His friend—yeah, he thought they were friends again, or still—answered on the second ring.

Jo HAD TO HELP Alan more than the other way around to descend the steep, rocky hillside. He muttered a few curses at his shoulder and the arm that he claimed was starting to come to life, but too damn slowly. He didn't hesitate to let her take some of his weight when that made sense.

Drew Frazier waited at the bottom for them, leaning against a department SUV. He had a second cop with him, not Deputy Hudson, thank goodness. Jo's instinctive distrust of Hudson was probably unfair, but his inclusion now would have made her uncomfortable.

"My place," Alan said as soon as Frazier reached out to clap him on his back. "We'll talk on the way. I've got to clean up a little."

He and she climbed in the back, dripping all over the seats and floor. Alan did most of the talking with Jo only chiming in as needed, mostly to explain the backstory of why she'd been so determined to explore the section of the cavern that her stepfather had made forbidden.

Drew called to have the road into the caverns blocked, then said, "I'll request a warrant while I'm waiting for you."

Naturally, Alan made light of his injuries, but she kept her mouth shut about those.

Ten minutes later, the SUV rocketed up Alan's dirt driveway and slammed to a stop in front of his house. He hustled her inside, said, "Only one bathroom. Once I'm out, it's all yours. I'll find some clothes that will do for you."

"Okay. I'll hurry."

And that's when he broke it to her that she was going to be left behind. It didn't matter what role she'd played thus far, how capable she was, she wasn't a cop, and wouldn't be allowed along on a police raid.

"*You're* not a lawman anymore!" burst out of her.

"Drew's trying to deputize me. Somebody has to lead them in."

"I could do that," she argued, "and I'm not the one who should be in the ER."

"Sorry." Voice and expression were adamant. Why had she bothered to waste her breath?

Furious, she was just as glad Alan and the other men were gone by the time she got out of the shower. If Lucy was alive, she'd need her sister, not a bunch of *cops*.

ALAN DIDN'T BLAME Jo for being royally ticked at being patted on the back and told she couldn't accompany them even as far as the cavern entrance. It wasn't fair, not after the courage she'd shown today, not when he knew she'd have followed orders. Maybe it was just as well that he was no longer in charge, though since the last thing he wanted was her in the line of fire again.

It was true that Drew needed one of them to lead them to the captured woman or women and to the bones. Reading Jo's glare, Alan appreciated her not having spoken up about how disabled he might be. Not finishing what he started wasn't in his genes.

He winced away from the thought that maybe Jo felt the same. She didn't have the same kind of background he did. He hated knowing how badly he'd screwed up, getting caught off guard like he had. The question of whether he'd made the wrong decision to run was going to eat at him forever if the killer had turned right around, because he had plenty of time, and killed another woman and maybe even his own daughter.

When Alan emerged from the house dressed in dry tactical boots, cargo pants and long-sleeve T-shirt, his gun on his hip, Drew waved at the back seat.

He drove as fast down the driveway as he had going the other way. Over his shoulder, he said, "Sheriff Robarts has officially deputized you."

In case Alan had to take an active role—say, in the event of a violent exchange with an unsub who could be a dangerous serial killer. He nodded his thanks.

A squad car was parked to block the turnoff to the cavern, while a second one hovered in wait for them. Alan appreciated the precaution. If any cops had driven in prematurely, there was the chance the sight would have panicked the killer if he hadn't already made a getaway. What if he grabbed a kid? He had nothing to lose at this point.

And that was based on the assumption that he either believed the cavers he'd pursued were strangers who had nothing to do with the investigation—or that there was no outlet from that lower level of the cavern. Or, hell, maybe he thought he'd taken care of them with that last spray of bullets.

The backup deputies peeled off toward the house.

When Alan, Drew and a deputy named Blake Norman walked into the gift shop, nobody who looked like Rod was in sight. A stranger manned the cash register and a long-haired guy who may have been a student was gathering a group for another tour.

Alan walked right to him. "Where's Rod Summerlin?"

Wide-eyed, the kid said, "I don't know. What's this about?"

"He's not leading a tour?"

"No, Brody has the one that's due back in—" he glanced toward a wall clock "—ten minutes."

"All right." Alan lowered his voice. "None of these folks will be going on a tour. Refund their money. We're halting operations for the rest of the day. Warn them they'll have to sit in their cars for a little while, too."

"But Rod has to make that decision—" He read Alan's hard stare just right and nodded.

Hands on the butts of their guns, Drew and one of the other deputies had disappeared down a short hall toward what were presumably offices and restrooms. They reappeared only moments later, shaking their heads.

Alan hadn't seen Rod Summerlin's truck in the parking lot. His tension ratcheted up. Was it possible they hadn't locked the barn door soon enough?

The guy at the register was issuing refunds to people who seemed more curious than mad. "I don't know what this is about," he kept saying.

Somewhere in there, the two other deputies walked in to let them know no one was answering the door at the house, a dog was barking frantically inside and no vehicles were parked there, either in the garage or next to it. Drew instructed one of the two to search the parking lot for Rod's truck, and he trotted out.

As tense as he'd ever been before any operation, Alan could *feel* each second ticking past. He understood why they were holding back; they couldn't let a bunch of tourists get caught up in a risk of being shot or grabbed. But he didn't like having to wait.

He heard the returning group before he saw them.

Brody appeared first, caught his eye right away and hustled up to him. "Why are there a bunch of cops here?"

"Your operation is shut down for the day. You need to tell your group that the gift shop is closed, and they should return to their cars."

He expected an argument that didn't come. Brody made his announcement along with an apology. And explained how everyone on the staff needed to help with an active police investigation. They'd be free to leave as soon as possible.

Once he locked the front door behind the last family of tourists, Brody whirled. "Does this have to do with Lucy?"

"What do you know?" Drew asked.

"She's gone." He sounded the next thing to frantic. "Dad was really furious this morning. Jo isn't here, either, but she let us know she'd be visiting a friend today. I wondered, though—" He broke off.

"Wondered?" Alan prodded.

"If she wasn't lying. It's like she knew something she wasn't saying. Things have been...really tense around here lately."

"You were right. Jo is responsible for gathering the information that got us a warrant for this raid," Alan said right out. "She wanted to be here, but we couldn't allow that. She's safe, though."

"Lucy?" The boy's eyes searched Alan's.

The best he could do was say, "We don't know."

At the request for a key to the lock on the gate, Brody

shook his head. "I don't know where Dad's been keeping it."

Alan bet there were a couple of copies, one on Dad's keychain. In fact...what if Lucy had taken her father's keys? He'd have noticed they were missing immediately.

"Do you know where your father is?"

"No. He's been...strange today." He frowned. "Mostly in his office, I think."

"His truck doesn't appear to be here. Did you see him leave?"

"No. Maybe somebody else did?"

But it turned out none of the employees had seen their boss in hours, which wasn't a surprise. There weren't enough of them to notice Rod's truck passing from the house unless someone had happened to glance out a window at the right time. Drew left two deputies behind with Brody and the other employees. Their instructions were to keep a sharp lookout for Rod returning in his truck.

Where the hell was that truck? The question stuck like a burr in Alan's mind. Jo's stepfather sure hadn't driven it into the cavern. Was there any chance at all they could have been wrong about who had chased them through the darkness?

He couldn't see it, though.

Summerlin could be on the run. Knowing his obsession with the family name and this damned cavern, Alan had trouble believing that, either. Rod had to know how hard it was to disappear, and that he'd be leaving everything he cared about behind. Still, they needed to check his bank accounts.

Watching Drew and Deputy Norman apply the bolt cutters to get the padlock off the gate, Alan pushed back at worry that would distract him from the moment. Once the gate swung open, the others stepped aside to allow him to take the lead. The silence felt ominous, even though he hadn't expected to hear any crying from here. Still—Rod had had time to kill Amy and—or—Lucy.

Not far in, Alan murmured to Drew, "Pretty sure from Jo's description that this is where the Summerlin kids held their parties." Drew turned his head to examine the room with the lamp attached to his borrowed helmet. Water shimmered in the light.

Only minutes later, Alan heard a whimper. He stiffened, as he was sure the other two men did. All three drew their weapons before Alan led the way, bent over—into a tight passage.

DESPITE HAVING BECOME aware that her entire body ached, Jo didn't think she could bear to just sit here. Alan's house was bare. A recliner sat in front of a TV, but what was she going to do, watch talk shows? Find something to read on the cinder block shelves she'd been surprised to see in his bedroom? Since her phone had been left behind, Alan couldn't even call her with news.

She rolled up the too-large borrowed sweatpants a bunch of times and still had to clutch the waist to be sure they didn't fall down as she paced. Her route led her to the front window in the stark living room. She could just see the corner of the new garage, which was when she was struck by the reminder that the one thing she *did* have was her car. She'd left the keys beneath the mat.

What would it hurt to drive over to the cavern entrance and wait for the men to reemerge? Surely Brody was there, even if the employees had been sent home. She was desperate to know what was happening, to *be* there if Lucy was led out alive. What Lucy needed should come first, even if Jo would be betraying Alan's trust that she'd do as he asked—or, in this case, ordered.

Damn it, either Lucy was alive, or she wasn't. Jo knew Alan would come back for her as quickly as he could.

Groaning, she went to explore those bookshelves after all, even though she couldn't imagine any story, however riveting, distracting her from this agony of waiting. But she chose a book and sat down at the kitchen table. She tried to read. She did. She even poured herself a glass of lemonade and sipped at it. The whole while, she waited tensely for the sound of a vehicle coming up to the house.

The stupid clock on the stove wasn't working, and it looked like the one on the microwave hadn't been set. She could measure the passage of time, though. Fifteen minutes. Half an hour. An hour. And she'd thought time crawled during their journey through the cavern.

Glass shattered at the front of the house. On a lightning bolt of adrenaline, she jumped to her feet. Someone was breaking in!

She raced for the back door and bounded off the porch. Grabbing again to hold up the sweatpants, she ran for all she was worth. If she could get to the car—

The man coming from the front of the house was cutting her off. Automatically measuring distances, Jo knew she wouldn't be fast enough. Then a gun shot tore up lawn right in front of her feet, breaking her stride, stealing precious seconds from her.

He plowed into her as if he were a linebacker, and she crashed down onto her face, his greater weight pinning her. Jo still thrashed and fought wildly, until something jammed into her neck.

The barrel of a gun.

Pretend to be surprised. Innocent, just as Alan had.

"Who are you? What are you doing?" she cried.

"You know who I am," her stepfather said, voice guttural. His chest heaved up and down. "And what I'm *doing* is figuring out the most satisfying way to kill you."

Rage took over. "You killed my mother!"

"Yes, I did. It's too bad I didn't take care of you then, too, but you were too handy. Now you've ruined everything."

It was Alan's hard face she saw when she closed her eyes and thought, *I'm dead.*

Chapter Sixteen

The men moved quietly. They hadn't really needed Alan's lead; it wasn't hard to follow the sound of hopeless crying. Ironic that it filled Alan with exhilaration. They were in time. Something good would come out of this. The knowledge was sweet, after his last police operation.

He was able to straighten at an intersection that wasn't quite a room. Turning left, he had to duck again. He moved now with his Glock held in firing position, his right hand barely supporting the left. A stench reached his nostrils, stronger than the whiffs he realized he'd been smelling for a couple of minutes.

In mere steps, he reached a much larger open space, sweeping it at gunpoint before allowing himself to focus on the two women staring at him. No, girls. Both were manacled to bolts driven into the wall. One was naked, bruised and emaciated, sitting in as close to a fetal position as she could get. The other wore jeans and a sweatshirt. One side of her face was discolored and swollen, the eye barely a slit.

"Lucy?" he asked.

She burst into tears. "You found us! We thought… earlier…"

"That was your sister and me," he said as gently as possible. "Was it your father who was here?"

Her face crumpled as she nodded.

The poor kid. "Bad luck he happened to be here. We had to circle around to get out of the cave so we could make a call."

He tipped his head toward Drew. "Lucy Summerlin."

"You're Deputy Frazier," she mumbled.

Shock not entirely hidden, Drew nodded kindly. "I can't tell you how glad I am to see you two girls." He'd lowered the small pack he carried and now took out a space blanket that he wrapped around the other young woman, who had fallen mute. "Amy Kendall?" he asked, voice soft, even though he, like Alan, had to recognize her from the photo plastered all over town.

Tears ran down her cheeks.

"Your family is going to be really glad to see you," Drew said.

Lucy watched, something fierce on her face that Alan recognized from her sister. She'd have done anything to protect Amy. In a way, that's what she'd done, he thought.

She ignored Deputy Norman, who appeared horrified but was bringing out the bolt cutters. "Where is my father?"

Alan squatted in front of her. "That was going to be my next question. When did you last see him?"

"He chased after you," she said. "We heard gunshots. When he came back, I thought he was going to kill us. He kept saying he was." A shudder rattled her. "He got mad at me a lot, but—"

Seeing her bewilderment, he gripped her knee. "He's your father."

"Except…" Lucy raised her gaze, filled with tumult, to his. "He said he killed my mother."

"Yeah. He did." There'd be time to talk, but this wasn't it. "What happened after he came back?"

Her lashes fluttered. "He said…he said maybe everything would be all right. He thought he'd taken care of some cavers who stumbled in here. He was going to go find out."

"Could you tell which way he went?"

She nodded. "His light was on. You know? He went right out of here."

"Back toward the entrance."

Leaving these traumatized girls in complete darkness. Alan had never hated anyone more. Still, he managed to sound calm. "Okay." He stood and turned to Drew. "You heard?"

"I heard. Howard? You go back and call for medics. Ask for a BOLO on Summerlin's truck, and more uniforms to surround this place. You can find your way out, can't you?"

Consumed by urgency and fear that he shouldn't have left Jo not only alone but unarmed, Alan suggested, "Why don't I go instead? I need to be sure Jo is okay."

Alarm transformed his friend's face as he understood immediately. They should have planned for all the eventualities if Rod wasn't here.

"Go. No, wait. Here's my keys. Call as soon as you get a signal."

"Will do." Alan caught the tossed set of keys and started for the arched opening. "I'll tell Brody Summerlin to wait to lead the other responders in."

Lucy's voice followed him. "Dad—he kept talking about Jo. Saying this was her fault. If he found her—"

A lump in Alan's throat kept him from answering. He only nodded before leaving, moving faster than was safe in passages that hadn't been cleared for the benefit of tourists.

The certainty that Jo needed him made him crazy.

"WHERE'S BURKE?" ROD pushed the gun barrel harder into her neck. "Was that the two of you in there?"

What was to be gained by not telling him the truth now? Jo thought. At least she could scare him, damage his God delusion.

"Yes. We called 9-1-1 as soon as we got out. He's gone with several deputies to free Lucy."

Rod wrenched her onto her back. "Maybe she's dead," he snarled.

"You'd kill your own daughter?" That was the hardest part to understand.

"I didn't want to."

Grief swept Jo. That sounded as if he'd already done it. "You're a monster."

"None of this would have happened if your mother hadn't tried to leave me."

"Oh, there's an excuse." She made no effort to hide her contempt.

He backhanded her, and her head rocked sideways, pain exploding over her cheekbone.

"If I'd been married, I'd never have gone out looking."

Dear God, how could he justify his evil, even to the point of being willing to kill his own child? But this time, Jo kept her mouth shut.

His eyes narrowed. "How'd you get out of the cavern? I've explored that level. There's no way."

"Obviously, there is. Alan explored all the local caves as a boy. He has a good memory, too. He led us straight out."

"That's not possible." His voice had risen.

"It is, if you're willing to trust yourself to the water and hold your breath for long stretches." In a bitter way, she almost enjoyed saying that. Rod had claimed to be the great cave explorer, but he couldn't swim. He'd have never considered sump diving, or even the far more tame way they'd floated out of the cave.

He swore viciously. "How long ago did he leave?"

"Like I'd tell you," she spat.

Jo desperately calculated. Would it occur to Alan, once Rod's absence became apparent, that he might come *here*?

Please, she begged silently. *Please let him be on his way back right now.*

As he emerged from the cavern, Alan paused only long enough to grip Brody's arm. "Your sister is alive. She's going to need you." When the boy started to turn, Alan shook his head. "Medics are on their way. They'll need you to lead them in. Can you do that?"

"Where—?"

"Not that far past the party cave. Take the middle passage. You'll smell waste and hear voices."

The young face hardened, and Brody nodded.

Then Alan dialed dispatch, passing on all the necessary information even as he ran to Drew's department vehicle, threw himself in, and put the car in gear. Ignoring the crackle of voices on the police radio, he accelerated with dangerous speed from the parking lot and along a road with virtually no shoulder separating his lane from a several hundred-foot plunge to the river.

Almost to his driveway, he saw the hood of what he recognized as Rod's old pickup truck barely visible in the single turnoff on this stretch of winding road above the river. He wouldn't have missed seeing it on their way to the cavern if it had been there. Right now, Alan didn't care where Rod had been in the interim, only what he'd find when he reached home. Should he drive in with siren screaming? Call for backup now that he knew Rod was here? Park and sneak in?

Making a decision, he drove a short distance up the driveway, then pulled to the side and parked. He called dispatch again and explained that the man they were hunting was here, at his house, and likely holding Jo Summerlin hostage.

"I'm sneaking in for a look. If I get a chance to take him down, I'll do it," he said bluntly. "But I want backup as soon as possible. Have them come in quietly, spread out around the yard. Sirens and the sound of an engine might trigger him to kill her."

"Yes, sir," the dispatcher said. "It's…really Rod Summerlin?"

"It is."

He ended the call while she was asking another question. Alan took the Remington rifle from the rack in the department vehicle, grabbed a box of ammunition, then set off up the driveway at a jog. Before the tree line, he veered to the left, thinking he might be able to approach using the cover of his pickup and Jo's car as well as the skeleton of the garage and the piles of lumber. The trees grew closer to the house from this direction, too.

An angry voice drifted to him.

God. Jo had to still be alive. Who else would that bastard be berating? They had to be outside, too, which might be bad news, depending on where they were. He could have sneaked into the house—

Then he saw them, the stocky man pinning Jo down right in the middle of the lawn. He had a gun in his hand, the barrel pressed against her neck. Scared to death, Alan realized the SOB would see or hear any approach.

Handguns weren't accurate from any great distance.

Despite the firestorm of emotion building in his chest, Alan remained capable of the detachment to calculate in an entirely familiar way. Unless something changed in the near future—Rod drew Jo to her feet and shoved her toward the house, cavern entrance or head of the driveway—it wouldn't be possible to cuff and arrest him. Alan's best option was to set up with the rifle.

Which would be doable only if his arm would stretch out in front of him…and if he had enough nerve and muscle control to squeeze the trigger gently with the index finger of a hand he could hardly feel.

He'd practiced with the Glock in his left hand plenty of times, but never with a sniper rifle. He had respectable skills with the rifle, but he'd always worked with a team that included one or two exceptional sharpshooters.

Who weren't here.

Okay. Where was the closest he could set up without drawing Rod's attention?

Alan scanned the familiar yard with the eye of a navy SEAL moving on his target.

STAGGERING, FALLING TO her knees again, Jo kept talking. This was her only possible tactic for delay. "Why did you ask me to come back for the summer?" If only she could get him to lower the gun…

Renewed rage lit on her stepfather's square-jawed face. "Because I thought you might be able to make Lucy see sense, of course! Some damn fantasy, and she won't hear about anything else!"

"Was it a fantasy?"

His laugh was even more unnerving than his visible anger. "The crying?"

"And the skull."

"I dragged that stupid deputy as far into the cavern

as his nerve would let him go, and we didn't find a thing. Why would my own daughter think I'm lying?"

Because you were?

"Because there was a skull," she ventured to say. "Rusty must have found it."

He stared at her. "The dog? What was he doing in there?" Rod showed his teeth. "Don't tell me they were that stupid!"

Then she wouldn't.

He let loose of a long string of expletives.

"Where is the skull?"

His shoulders moved. "Tossed it in with the others."

The same place her body would go if he had his way—but in this, he didn't. Had he yet grasped that he'd reached the end?

Of course he had. The look in his eyes was answer enough. He intended to savor killing her, the stepdaughter he had never wanted who he now believed had bulldozed the construction of his twisted life.

But she also saw his uneasiness when he scanned their surroundings, not liking how exposed they were.

"Move it!" he snapped, yanking her to her feet and shoving her forward, his body almost pressed to her back so he could keep the gun in position.

Were they heading for the house? The cavern he believed should be his? Once in there, she'd have no hope of rescue.

Better to die quickly than let this monster possibly rape her before he put a bullet in her head, and then his own.

She stumbled, crying out. "You're hurting me."

A hideous expression on his face, he ground the barrel of the gun harder into her cheek until she whimpered involuntarily.

"You want to die *now*? Is that it?"

No, she didn't want to die, but even less did she want to give him any satisfaction whatsoever. He'd killed her mother and very likely her sister, stolen her family from her. Jo summoned all her rage and hate so as to be ready for the smallest mistake on his part that would let her take him off balance.

ALAN HAD TO WAIT until they disappeared into the house before he ran, staying inside the edge of the woods until he reached the back. The door stood open; he bet Jo had fled out that way when she heard Summerlin coming in the front.

Seeing no movement in the back windows, he took a chance and sprinted for the back porch, where he pressed himself to one side of the door. He carefully leaned the rifle against the wall; it would be no use to him in close quarters.

A voice came to him. Jo's.

"If you just hadn't grabbed Amy, none of this would have happened. I mean, Lucy was already up in arms, I was home… What were you thinking?"

Alan clenched his jaw. Was she baiting this bastard because she thought she could keep him talking, or because it gave her courage? Maybe even satisfaction?

Don't let it backfire.

Her stepfather did say something in return, his rumble harder to make out. Alan could tell they weren't in the kitchen, though, so he gripped his Glock in his left hand, braced it with his barely responsive right, and slipped into the house.

He'd learned which floorboards squeaked, so he was able to move swiftly and silently across the room. The pained sound Jo let out allowed Alan to pinpoint their location. Living room.

Two more steps, peering around the corner, he saw them.

Summerlin mostly had his back to Alan. The side of Jo's face he could see was swollen. She wouldn't see him.

What would the SOB do if Alan challenged him? Whirl to shoot at him? Or shoot Jo?

Alan waited. He'd been known for his patience, once upon a time, but when Jo was the one in danger...

Moving with shocking speed, she grabbed her stepfather's arm and shoved it up until the gun almost pointed at the ceiling. Alan took his chance even as she seemed to be trying to knee Summerlin in the groin at the same time.

"Police!" He stepped into the room. "Hands in the air!"

With a snarl, Summerlin tore free from her grip and turned the barrel of his gun downward. Toward her. Alan pulled the trigger.

One shot was all it took.

AT THE CRACK of a gunshot, Jo could only struggle to understand why there was no pain. The next instant, Rod's body fell into hers, blood everywhere.

Screaming, she shoved at him, rolled out from under the weight, freezing when she could see his ruined head.

"Jo!" Roaring her name, Alan gave an extra push to free her from Rod.

"Alan?"

He dropped to his knees next to her, paying no attention to her stepfather's body only a foot or two away. She had never even dreamed of seeing a look on his face so frantic, as if losing her would have been unendurable.

She reached for his hand. "You shot him."

"I did. *God.*" He seemed to want both hands to tear open her shirt, then his fingers to thread through her blood-soaked hair. "You're hurt. Where are you hurt?"

"I'm not." Aches and bruises didn't count. "I'm not. He was going to kill me, but I think he wanted to—"

He could tell she didn't want to say the words, and finally did grip her hand. Hard. "I guessed. That's probably the only thing that kept you alive long enough for me to get here."

Jo made herself sit up. "Did you find them?" Her throat tried to clog. "The bodies?"

"We didn't get as far as the bones. I came back as soon as we found your sister and Amy Kendall, Jo. They're alive."

"He told me he'd killed them."

Alan shook his head. "Amy isn't in good shape, but she's young. Given a lot of help, she'll make it back." Something almost like a smile lifted one corner of his mouth. "I think Lucy is mostly furious." He grimaced then. "In shock. Her dad told her he'd murdered her mother. That he had to kill her because she wouldn't let up. That's...all going to hit her sooner or later."

At a thunder of footsteps on the porch, she started, then realized a uniformed man had entered with a handgun held in firing position. Even as he lowered it, a sound from the back porch suggested a second officer would be on them any second. A siren came from the road, but continued on toward town.

"That's probably the ambulance." Alan sank onto his butt, looking exhausted.

And why wouldn't he be? For a moment, their day flashed through her mind: him intercepting her right in front of the cavern entrance, the long, confusing trip through the dark labyrinth, the bones, the confrontation with Rod, the gunshots and plummet into the hole. The eventual escape, and everything that had happened since.

"You need to go to the hospital," she said, aware of the two cops staring down at her dead stepfather.

"Yeah. I kind of guess there'll be a few questions, too." His eyes, still desperate, met hers. "Will you come with me?"

"This time, you couldn't stop me."

Epilogue

The first person Jo saw in the hospital waiting room
was her brother, who met her with outstretched arms.
His face showed the remnants of tears he didn't seem
to have noticed. "You're okay," he mumbled near her
ear. "Dad didn't find you?"

Her own eyes burning, she pulled back. "He did.
He's dead, Brody. Do you know what he did?"

Her brother nodded, his throat working. "I'm glad
he's dead. I'd have killed him myself if I could."

The three of them sat down and Jo told him about
the things Rod had said, and that Alan had shot him
to save her.

Brody held out a hand to Alan. "You saved both of
them."

Alan smiled crookedly. "I think your stubborn sister saved Lucy, at least." Then he grinned. "Both your
sisters seem to be stubborn, come to think of it."

Brody laughed, a little out of control, then let his
head fall forward and gripped his hair, pulling it hard.
"I can't believe all this."

"Where's Lucy?" Jo asked. "And…and Amy?"

"They're both back there. The nurses kicked me out, but I'll bet they'll let you go in," he told Jo. "Amy's parents are here."

Jo was momentarily distracted when an older uniformed police officer walked in, looking around. His face was familiar. She must have seen a photo. He came straight to Alan. "Can I have a word?"

"Sheriff." Despite Jo's hand darting out to stop him, Alan stood. He and the sheriff walked a distance away and talked for a few minutes, Jo watching him in alarm.

When she saw that blood had soaked through his shirt, she jumped up and went to him. "Excuse me. Alan was *shot* today. They'd better have three doctors working back there."

The sheriff looked startled by her militant tone, but nodded, his gaze lingering on Jo's face. She paid no attention, marching Alan up to the counter, then accompanying him as if it was her right when a nurse immediately escorted him back to an ER stall. But once they sat him on a bed in a cubicle, he said, "Go see your sister. She should come first."

"I'm…" Heaven help her, she was crying. Why now?

Alan smiled with tenderness that squeezed her heart. He held out his good hand to her. "They're going to need you, you know. Brody and Lucy."

They would. Jo had already realized that. She had a chance to make up for the years she'd stayed away. Tomorrow, she'd give her notice to the school district in Illinois and try to find a job locally. She didn't even have to ask to see that Alan understood. What scared her was wondering what he'd do.

"I'm not going anywhere," he said, as if reading her mind. "I need you, too."

She flung herself against him, held him while they exchanged strength and comfort, exactly as they'd done so many other times during this nightmare of a day, and wiped her tears and probably some snot on his already filthy shirt.

When she lifted her head, he studied her wet, blotchy, swollen face as if he didn't even notice the nurse or doctor who'd just pushed back the curtain to enter.

Voice husky, he said, "The sheriff hinted that I might replace the useless detective who was nearing retirement anyway. Even if that doesn't happen, we can make this work." Muscles flickered in his jaw. "You and me. Assuming…"

She didn't need him to finish the sentence. "There's nothing I want more." Ignoring the audience, she kissed him. Not very well, or for very long, but he looked satisfied, and she felt buoyed by hope when she rushed out to find her sister.

* * * * *

HARLEQUIN
PLUS

Announcing a **BRAND-NEW**
multimedia subscription service
for romance fans like you!

Read, Watch and Play.

Experience the easiest way to get
the romance content you crave.

Start your **FREE 7 DAY TRIAL** at
<u>www.harlequinplus.com/freetrial</u>.